LOVE BEYOND DESTINY

BOOK 11 OF MORNA'S LEGACY SERIES

BETHANY CLAIRE

Editor: Dj Hendrickson
Cover Designed by Damonza

Available In eBook, Paperback, Hardback, & Large Print Paperback

eBook ISBN: 978-1-947731-71-4
Paperback ISBN: 978-1-947731-72-1
Hardback ISBN: 978-1-947731-73-8
Large Print Paperback ISBN: 978-1-947731-94-3

For all of my readers,

For your patience. For your support. For reading.

PROLOGUE

Morna & Jerry's - Scotland - September - One Year After the Start of Our Story - Present Day

She wasn't supposed to be here. She'd promised him. She'd promised him to stay where she'd said goodbye to him.

But something had changed within her—he could feel it in every quick thump of his anxious pulse. She no longer cared about the promises she'd made to him. He no longer held a monopoly on her heart.

He'd known—hoped even—that in time she would come to love another, but why this man? Why another with magic? An ordinary man couldn't hurt her, but a man with magic could do whatever he wished, and his beloved would be powerless to stop him. How was he to know whether this stranger was worthy of her?

At least before, the distance between them was great enough that he could remain oblivious to her choices. But now, he could feel everything—every emotion—every contradiction. It was misery.

The nearness of her would end him. His mind tormented him

with agonizing memories of every decision that had brought him here—standing at the end of a narrow road leading to the home of a witch he knew wouldn't help him.

He had nothing left to lose. If she refused his request, he knew he wouldn't be able to stay away from her.

His strength was failing fast.

Each day he cared less for those whose lives rested in his beloved's hands.

"*M*orna, lass. There's a man at the end of the road. He keeps pacing as if he canna decide whether or not he wishes to approach our home. Do ye know him?"

She didn't, but the lad certainly knew of her. Otherwise, he would've been unable to see the magical inn.

"No, I canna say that I do. Nor did I see him coming." She sighed before continuing. "Sometimes it seems as if I am no longer as perceptive as I once was."

Reaching for her coat next to the door, she looked over her glasses at her husband's humored expression. "What do ye wish to say, Jerry?"

"O'course ye are not as perceptive. 'Tis only right that yer powers wane somewhat with age. If aging dinna impact ye in some way, 'twould be dreadfully unfair. Let me grab my own coat. I'll walk with ye to greet him."

"No." Now that she was aware of the man's presence, she could feel him acutely. "'Tis fine, truly. I doona yet know what this man needs, but I know there is nothing ye can do for him. Go and take a bath in that new walk-in, jetted tub of yers."

Jerry stood and wiggled both brows mischievously at her. "When he leaves will ye join me? There's plenty of room for two."

Laughing, she reached for Jerry as he passed and gently pressed her lips to his.

"I'd love to, but I've the feeling this willna be a short visit. If ye wait that long, ye shall be wrinkled as a prune by the time I make it upstairs."

"I'm already verra prune-like, lass."

She laughed unwillingly, the sudden bout of laughter helping to ease the knot which had settled in her chest at the sight of the man outside.

Perhaps Jerry saw himself that way, but every time she looked at her husband, she could only see the young man he'd once been. He was her favorite thing to look at in all the world.

"I love every wrinkle ye've got. Now go—one of us should enjoy the evening."

Morna waited until she could hear the water running through the pipes above her before opening the door and stepping out into the brisk evening air. The stranger saw her immediately and stopped his pacing as he straightened and looked at her as she approached.

"'Twill be dark soon, lad. If ye've business here, 'tis best ye come inside and see to it."

Under different circumstances, the stranger would've been handsome. But now, with his sad and strained gaze, his dark blue eyes were bloodshot and swollen. He appeared as if he'd been awake for a week straight and that for most of that time he'd been crying.

"Are ye Morna?"

"Aye." Morna extended her hand to him. "'Tis me ye wished to see, is it not? Tell me yer name and follow me inside."

Morna didn't miss the man's hesitation. She knew right away the name he gave her would not be the name given to him at birth.

"Bechard. Ye may call me Bechard."

Morna smiled to herself as she turned her back to him and motioned gently for him to follow.

"'Tis not the loveliest alias ye could have chosen."

She sensed the man stop behind her, and she looked back over her shoulder to ease his fear. "Doona worry, lad. If ye wish to keep yer real name to yerself, I suppose ye've reason to do so. Hang yer coat next to the door and have a seat in the living room. I'll fetch us some tea, then we will get about whatever business has brought ye here."

Bechard slowly took one step inside Morna's home.

"'Twas my father's name."

The man—she couldn't bring herself to think of him as Bechard since she knew it was not his real name—carried magic not unlike her own. The air around him was thick with it. Morna suspected that even mortal humans could sense it in his presence, though few would be able to explain what they felt while around him.

The man's magic—like the opposite side of a coin to her own—was of druid origin. It was easy at her age, after all of her experience, to place where one's powers came from. But while this man's source was evident, his purpose was not. Most druids—indeed, all she'd ever known—were beholden to a purpose. This man seemed entirely alone. He had to be. For if there were anyone else he could've gone to for help, she had no doubt he would be there now. Why go to a stranger for something that was clearly so personal to him?

Staring perhaps a little too long, she jumped at the sound of the pipes creaking as Jerry turned off the running water upstairs. Jarred back to the present and to the stranger's last admission, she pointed to one of the two empty chairs next to the fire and spoke. "Ah, that explains the odd choice of name. Well, pity to him then. Go and sit. I'll be just a moment."

The use of magic for boiled water was a frivolous thing, but she allowed herself the indulgence. The man's nerves seemed perilously close to shattering. She feared if she left him alone for more than a moment, she would return to see him collapsed on the floor of her living room, swallowed by his misery.

After first reaching for the smallest of her teacups, she thought again, and reached for the ones reserved for especially gloomy days. Gathering all she needed, she made her way back toward the man. He turned at the sound of her approach. Morna looked into his eyes and sighed as a bit of the tension in her own chest relaxed just a little. A bit of the panic in the man's gaze had subsided. He was ready to talk.

"I know that ye doona know me, but I am here to beg ye for help. I need ye to break the bond I share with another. 'Tis most urgent."

Nodding toward the tray upon the table so that he might begin to prepare his own cup, Morna relaxed into her chair.

"A bond? Ye know I shall need more than that, lad. 'Tis one of blood or kinship?" She hesitated and then shook her head, the memory of his strangled gaze flashing into her mind. "No, ye needn't answer. 'Tis a heart bond, aye?"

The man didn't stir or blow on his tea before slurping at the steaming cup he held in his hands. If it burned him, he showed no sign of it.

"Aye."

"Is it a bond of love or of marriage?"

Another slurp. Morna had to purse her lips together to keep from grinning at the way the man held his teacup. He cupped it like a bowl, as if there were no handle on its side.

Something inside the man's throat audibly caught and his answer was broken and choppy as he forced the words.

"Both. By God, 'tis both."

"Why then do ye wish to break yer bond with her? Does she no longer love ye?"

One last slurp and the man emptied his cup.

"She loves me still. And I love her more than I can bear. 'Tis why ye must help me to end this misery. 'Twas torturous enough when I had only my own grief to contend with, but now that she's here, I can feel her again."

His choice of words all but confirmed Morna's first suspicions about the strange man—he was not from this time. It explained the kinship she felt with the man's powers—they shared a gift for bending time.

"Ye mean in this time, aye?"

Setting the emptied cup down on the tray, he glanced up at Morna with weary eyes.

"Aye. The lass promised me she would stay. But she dinna do so. Now that she's here, 'tis as if my verra heart is being slowly poisoned. There is another now and he slowly heals her heart in a way that should be my doing. If our bond remains, I willna be able to stay away. I will go to her. I will take her back. I canna stand for another to hold her if I must be bound to feel it. Please, Morna, rid me of her. I canna bear this."

Morna sat quietly for a long moment, observing the man as he waited for her answer. Why would anyone voluntarily tear themselves away from someone they loved so much?

"I canna say aye when I doona understand. Ye must help me to see why ye would wish to do such a thing. Ye know that ending the bond willna truly take her from ye. Ye will still feel her loss, still grieve her."

The man nodded solemnly. "I know, but at least I willna be able to feel her heart alight when another man touches her. I willna be able to feel the way her breath comes short when she thinks of him. No one should have to endure such torture."

The man had chosen to ignore the first part of her statement, and she couldn't allow it to slide by. She couldn't, in good conscience, perform such a sorrowful act without knowing the motive behind him asking her to do so.

"I'll decide nothing until ye tell me yer story, lad."

The man stood, and Morna could see that the warm tea had done much to revive him. His shoulders were no longer slumped, and there was some fire in the way he scrubbed both hands over his face in frustration. He spoke to her through the small slit between his palms as he gripped at his face.

"If I tell ye, I know ye willna help me."

6

Her curiosity rising by the second, she settled more deeply into her chair.

"I'll not help ye unless ye tell me, either. So ye might as well do so and take yer chances."

Morna watched as the man took a deep, sorrowful breath before moving to sit across from her. She waited silently for him to begin.

"I grew up in a time not too distant from yer own. And like ye, I was born with powers. I was aware of what lay inside me much earlier than most who have magic. But as I am certain ye know, druid magic is different than what ye possess. Ye have more free will, less destiny, attached to yer choices."

Morna wasn't sure she agreed with the man's assessment of magic. Looking back on her own life, it seemed as if she'd been only a small piece of something much bigger than herself—something which was written long before she ever breathed her first breath.

"Less destiny, perhaps, but we still have a purpose we are bound to once we discover it."

The man dismissed her, shaking his head as he continued. "Mayhap so, but lass, I've always been a solitary creature. I wanted my own life, one filled with my own choices. I dinna want to be a part of anything. I dinna want to be a pawn in any greater purpose.

"When I was only a lad, word of a man seeking young men with magic spread among my clansmen. This stranger needed a group of druids young enough to train and strong enough to help him lock away an evil being on his isle. The moment I heard the man's story, I knew I was bound to it. Something inside me lit like a beacon welcoming the stranger, I knew it wouldna be long before he found me and recruited me into his group of eight lads he meant to use as protection."

"Was the man named Nicol Murray?" Whatever Morna expected the stranger's story to be, it certainly wasn't this.

"Aye."

7

"And where did ye grow up?"

Morna knew the man's answer before he gave it. A memory of her own from long, long ago had surfaced. Now everything seemed clear to her.

"Allen territory."

Hamish, Raudrich, the beginning of her own strange tie to The Isle of Eight all tied back to the stranger sitting in front of her now.

"Ah. So ye fled to the future and hid until another lad was chosen in yer place?"

The man straightened in his seat to look at her. "Aye. Was my story so predictable?"

"No, lad, but I am a part of this story whether ye know it or not. Hamish—I suspect he was probably laird when ye were young—and I were once verra close. He called to me as he prepared to die and asked me to look after his grandson, Raudrich, in whatever way I could. Ye see, lad, Raudrich had been called into The Eight by Nicol Murray, and Hamish desperately wanted me to aid his grandson to be set free from a life of duty and obligation. At the time, I thought it a concern that any grandfather might have, but now I see 'twas more than that.

"Hamish knew that all those with magic were born to a purpose. If The Isle of Eight was Raudrich's true purpose, then Hamish would've been glad to see his grandson fulfill it. But it wasn't Raudrich who was supposed to be there, 'twas ye, and Hamish knew it."

The man's eyes filled with tears. He gently closed them as they spilled over.

"Aye, I've no doubt he knew. Hamish always seemed to know everything. Raudrich was my closest friend. I dinna know I was dooming him to such a fate when I left. I was young. All I wanted was to be free. I canna tell ye how sorry I am for what my choices have done to others."

"Lad, doona be sorry. Mayhap Raudrich wasna destined to The

Isle before, but he certainly is now. I know if ye asked him, he would change nothing in his life."

Opening his eyes, the man briskly brushed away the tears. "That is some comfort, at least."

"Forgive me, lad, but I doona see how this story has anything to do with why ye came here."

"I am not yet finished. At the end of my story, it will all be abundantly clear to ye."

Morna nodded, urging him to carry on.

"After I left and came here to the twenty-first century, I grew up in Scotland. I found work with a farmer not too far from here. He allowed me to sleep in a converted space above his barn. I happily believed that even the ghastly smell which I breathed day in and day out was better than the life that awaited me back home.

"I returned occasionally to see my mother, who believed I'd found similar work only in my own time. She was relieved that my powers had yet to call me to some great and dangerous purpose, so she never questioned anything I told her verra much.

"At the age of thirty, the farmer I worked for died. His land was sold to a man who dinna wish to keep me on. I dinna mind. By that age, I was restless and ready to reinvent myself. I went to America and fell in love."

Morna couldn't help but smile, despite the gloomy nature of the man's story. Of course the man's wife was modern. Almost all of the women Morna meddled with were.

"With yer wife?"

"Aye. The moment I saw her, I was consumed. We fell for one another quickly. Before long, I told her the truth of my magic and where and when I was from. Shortly after we married, I visited my mother alone to tell her of the good news. It was then that I learned of Laird Allen's murder. I knew that Raudrich would have much to settle after his brother's death. After abandoning him to my fate once, I couldna leave him alone to handle this.

"So—after much convincing and preparation—I took my wife

and her father into the past. More quickly than I could've imagined, we settled into a happy life there. But it wasna long before my past caught up with me. I couldna outrun my destiny, no matter how much I tried."

With the man's story still unfinished, Morna said nothing as she reached out to give his hand a reassuring squeeze.

With another breath, he continued. "Raudrich told few within the village, but his loyalty was now pledged to The Isle of Eight. He couldna be laird. After some time home, he asked if I would take the land from him and serve as laird since he could not. It seemed a weighty decision. So, as many in our territory often do, I went to look into a pool of waters that can tell a man's future to see if mayhap my fate from so long ago had changed, and now I was meant to be laird of Allen Territory."

Morna was all too familiar with the magical waters of Allen territory. At one time in her life, they'd caused her more pain than she wished to remember.

"I canna imagine that went well, aye? Such waters are dangerous."

A painful sob escaped the man's chest, and Morna regretted interrupting his story.

"Aye, those damned waters have ruined my life."

"What did ye see?"

"It was not my future that I saw that day. Instead, I saw my wife and her place at The Isle of Eight Lairds. She is as tied to The Isle as I was meant to be. While I could choose to abandon my own destiny, I couldna deny my wife hers."

"So what did ye do?"

"I made her promise to remain in the seventeenth century and then I faked my death. I knew that with time she would be led to The Isle so she could fulfill her purpose there. For months she did as she promised, but something has brought her here now. I doona wish to be a bad man, Morna. I foiled fate once. I shouldna do it again.

"I've studied much about The Isle in this time. I know the legends. I know how Machara's bond over The Eight is supposed to end. My wife is meant to be one of the women to help destroy her, but my love for her is a selfish thing. If she is here, close enough that I can feel her, I willna be able to stay away. I will go to her. I will win her back, and I will keep her here, far from The Isle, damning everyone who lives there. I no longer care what happens to them. This pain within me is too much. All I want is for it to end, either by ye breaking this bond so I may mourn her in peace or by holding her in my arms once again."

Her heart heavy, Morna leaned forward to answer him. "I'm sorry, lad. I canna do as ye wish."

"Why? How can ye not? Ye must see how important this is. If ye doona help me, people will die. History will change."

"'Tis not that I doona wish to help ye. I do. But I canna do so. If ye know all that ye say ye do about The Isle, ye know that magic canna be used to defeat Machara. It must be mortal women that destroy her. Yer wife doesna know that ye live. By removing yerself from her life, by leaving her no choice about whether she wishes to fulfill her destiny at The Isle or remain with ye, ye have already intervened with magic. If I were to sever yer bond without her knowing, 'twould again be magic. She must be the one who decides what sort of life she wishes to live."

Morna watched as desperation crept back into his gaze. He stood and began to pace around the room.

"If I go to her, she will choose me."

"What makes ye so sure? Ye said yerself that there is another."

"She possesses every bit of my soul. How could I not possess as much of hers?"

"I doona doubt that at one time ye did, but ye underestimate the heart's ability to expand, lad. While ye lived, ye were her everything. I am sure, now that she believes ye are gone, she loves ye no less than she ever did, but ye canna be everything to anyone once ye are in the ground. It serves no one to devote one's life to those who are gone. After she has grieved ye, she must make room for more."

When he stared back at her blankly, the frustration in his gaze said all that his words did not.

Morna continued, "That's the way with hearts. Sometimes ye think it willna ever be able to hold such love again, to hold more than it once did, but its ability to open is infinite. More love can always come in. With time, even though her love for ye will never fade, her heart will grow larger. Someone else can saturate her soul, too. Maybe someone else already has."

Anger flashed in the man's eyes, and for a moment, Morna thought the man might lunge at her.

"I will take her back. She is mine as long as this bond remains. 'Tis why I need ye to break it."

Morna shrugged. Each moment spent in this man's presence allowed her to see him more clearly. He was a man unsure of everything. A man with so much to learn.

"Mayhap so. If ye are sure that ye canna move on with the bond ye share still inside ye, then even if I break it, yer business with her willna be finished. Go to her. Tell her what ye must. If she agrees to break the bond, then I shall break it."

"She willna agree. She will choose me."

Morna stood. Tired and eager to be in Jerry's arms, all she wanted was for the young man to leave. She couldn't know if she was making the biggest mistake of her life, but she knew what this stranger didn't seem to understand—that none of this was for them to decide. She could meddle in love, but she couldn't meddle in fate, and this time it involved more than a handful of hearts.

"Perhaps, but ye forget that she's already grieved for ye. Do ye not think she will feel betrayed when ye show up in her life again? 'Tis cruel what ye've done to her."

The man followed closely as she walked to her front door.

"She will forgive me. She will choose me, and the future of The Isle will be ruined. People we both know and love will die."

Opening the door, she ushered him out into the cool evening air, before closing the door with her parting words.

"Ye may be right, but it doesna matter. The choice *must* be hers. Ye and I are just chess pieces in this game. Everything depends on her."

CHAPTER 1

*A*llen Territory - 1651

*T*he widow's theatrics did nothing to hide the satchels filled to the point of bursting with her late husband's belongings. Candlesticks, linens, goblets—anything that would sell for a fair price—bulged inside the three large bags lying against the wall.

"I canna thank ye enough for coming to offer me comfort. 'Tis truly..." The woman paused as she pinched her eyes closed, narrowed her nostrils and forced tears to come before throwing her arms around my neck for the fifth time since I'd arrived. "I canna breathe without him. And ye...ye are the only one who truly understands."

Dutifully, I patted the charlatan on the back. For today, I was still the primary landowner in Allen Territory and such a visit was necessary. She was right—I did understand grief. It was something I contended with each and every day—a constant companion that never left.

Keeara wasn't grieving for anyone. If the state of her home was any indication, I'd wager she'd helped the old man to his grave. I'd even double the bet that by nightfall, she and all of the home's belongings would be gone from this village for good.

"Aye. I know 'tis difficult to lose someone ye love." Peeling her off me, I stepped away and toward the door. "I simply wished to come and express my sympathy. Everyone in the village is happy to offer support however we can. For now though, I must go."

She said nothing until I stepped just outside her home. Until that point, I thought perhaps I could make it through the torturous encounter without saying something regretful. Her last words to me quickly dissolved any hope of that.

"I can still feel him. At night when I sit down at the table we shared together, I sometimes feel his hands upon my shoulders and his lips against my cheek. I believe he wishes to remind me that I'm not alone. That he's still here tending to me the best way he can."

Since Ross' death, I'd yearned to feel him. But my pleading and hoping never did anything to bring about his presence. If my Ross —my beloved Ross—wasn't going to stick around to look after me, then the stranger Keeara had married certainly wasn't going to either.

Looking back over my shoulder, my irritation with her charade unleashed itself.

"Come now, Keeara. The man was older than yer father. Ye'd been married a week and ye only met a fortnight ago. I doona care that ye dinna love him. But doona make a mockery of those who did love and truly lost it."

The feigned expression of agony eased on Keeara's face. Guiltily, she gave me a nod before closing the door behind me.

I couldn't bring myself to take my normal route back home. Today, the walk through the middle of the village back to the castle simply seemed too public. With my successor and his men settling in throughout the territory, I knew I'd be met with questions and the usual concerns that come with introducing people to someone new, and I didn't have the energy to deal with it today.

Instead, I took the route through the woods, along a worn and clearly marked trail, taken by many of those that had lived in the castle through the centuries. It provided some sort of shielded respite from socializing if one simply wasn't up to acting as "laird" for the afternoon.

I always enjoyed the sound of branches and leaves cracking beneath my feet. Even after years of living here, the soft crunch provided a sense of grounding I rarely had in my life before coming here.

"Halt. If ye be a lady, please stay back just a moment. If a man, ye may proceed."

"Raudrich?" The distinct deep bellow of my friend's voice was recognizable anywhere, but I'd not expected to hear it again for some time. I stayed back as instructed and did my best to pretend that I couldn't hear him peeing just a few steps from me.

Once finished, he turned toward me with a smile.

"Silva, 'tis good to see ye, lass. Forgive my rudeness. I knew that once I breached the gates of the castle, Griffith would pull me away and I wouldna have the opportunity to relieve myself until bedtime."

"What are ye doing here? Yer letter only said that my replacement was arriving in a fortnight, not ye."

Falling in step beside me, we walked together until Raudrich reached his horse. Rather than mounting the great beast, he grabbed its reins and led the horse beside us as we talked.

"I dinna intend to come when I wrote the letter, but then I thought mayhap 'twould make it easier on all involved if I came to help with the transition."

"Last time ye did that, ye ended up staying far longer than ye intended."

The youngest of the two Allen sons, Raudrich grew up believing that Allen territory would never fall to him, but after the devastating murder of his brother, Raudrich returned to his home with the intention of finding a man suitable to relinquish his land to. He easily decided on my husband Ross, but only three days after the decision was announced, my husband died.

Out of duty, Raudrich remained home, even though his loyalty was now pledged to another clan. He waited for another worthy of the responsibility to come along for some time, but when the cost of being away from his druid brothers on The Isle of Eight Lairds began to take its toll, he was forced to leave. In his haste, he deeded all his land to me.

"Aye, though 'twill not be necessary this time. I leave for home the day after tomorrow."

We walked in silence until we reached the castle gates. Once there, Raudrich reached out and gently squeezed my arm. "I am sorry for what I did to ye, Silva. I dinna know my decision would cause ye such misery. I truly believed ye would thrive here."

"Ye needn't be sorry. 'Twas not the duties of laird that brought me misery. 'Tis only that I doona know how to be here without Ross. I wanted to leave even before ye gave me the land. Ye trapped me here, but o'course ye couldna have known that."

He shook his head in disagreement. "Had I taken the time to truly speak to ye, I woulda known. I shoulda asked ye if ye wanted it. I have made certain this time that the next person to take over Allen territory desires such a position. What do ye think of Griffith?"

"In truth, I only know him from the days we spent together while journeying with Sydney to yer home. From what I've seen, I believe he will do a fine job with these people, though I suspect he has much growing up to do."

Raudrich laughed and nodded in agreement. "Aye. 'Tis true of all men."

As if summoned by our words, Griffith appeared at the other end of the courtyard. I smiled at Raudrich before excusing myself. I had already fallen prey to Griffith's penchant for stealing one's whole day with unexpected conversation and activity, and I desperately wanted to spend my last afternoon and evening in the master bedchamber of the castle deciding what was going to be the next chapter in my life.

As a reluctant caretaker for the people of Allen Territory, it hadn't taken me long to find all of the quietest stairways and hallways to sneak around the castle unnoticed, so it took me no time to reach the room that would soon be Griffith's. Opening the door, I stepped inside and smiled at the sight I intuitively knew I would find—my new stepsister sprawled out across my bed, her feet hanging off the end as she held a book up into the air as she read.

"I thought ye might need some help loading yer belongings into trunks."

She gently set the book down and rose from her horizontal position to smile at me as I walked over to the bed and teasingly pinched her big toe.

"That and ye wished to escape yer younger siblings for a bit, aye?"

She shrugged and swung her body forward as she sprang from the bed. "Perhaps. Silva, ye do know that ye are back in yer bedchamber now, aye? With only me to hear ye speak, ye doona need to use the accent."

My passable-at-best Scottish brogue had become part of my identity for so long that I always found it difficult to slip back into my real skin.

Few people knew the truth of who I was. Silva Broun, keeper of a seventeenth century Scottish territory in the northernmost part of the Highlands was truly a twenty-first century American who fell in love with an extraordinary man and out of her own time.

CHAPTER 2

"*Y*ou're right." Smiling in Olivia's direction, I relaxed my neck, rolled my head from side to side and shook out my shoulders. "It's necessary so much of the time that it just sticks. Sometimes I feel as if my American accent is the one I'm faking."

Olivia laughed and shook her head. "No, I can assure ye that yer American accent sounds much more genuine. I doona know how no one has ever questioned yer Scottish one."

"They have no reason to. The truth wouldn't even occur as a possibility to most people I know."

"What about Raudrich? Both his best friend and his wife are time travelers as ye are. How did he never see it?"

"For most of the time that I've known Raudrich, his life has been in chaos. When we first met, he'd just lost his brother. Then Ross passed away, and not long after, Raudrich's sight began to fail as a result of him being separated from the other members of The Eight and he was forced to leave here. I don't think he had the time or energy to question anything outside of what was going on in his own world. I don't blame him for that."

"Ye are right."

Olivia sighed and took a step forward to wrap her arms around me. She was twenty years old, but she still seemed like such a child.

"Silva, may I tell ye something?"

"Of course you can."

"I'm coming with ye when ye leave here."

Olivia wasn't going anywhere, but I saw no need to shatter her dreams without first hearing her out.

"You are? Does your mother know this?"

Olivia groaned, stepped away from me, and dramatically threw herself backwards on the bed.

"Why does she need to know? Did ye ask yer father's permission for everything ye did when ye were my age? Most of the women I grew up with are already married with three bairns hanging off them. When my own mother was my age, I was six years old."

I shuddered thinking about Leanna's situation—not that it was unusual in this time, but my new stepmother was only six years older than myself, and she'd already birthed seven children. The fact that five of them still lived put her in the lucky minority of most mothers in this time.

"No, I didn't, but I did at least inform him of my plans most of the time."

"Ah-ha." She sat up and held up one finger as if to let me know that she had me exactly where she wanted me. "Ye just said *most. Most* of the time ye spoke to him of yer plans. Not all. *Most* of the time, I do tell my mother things, but I doona wish to tell her this."

I mimicked her earlier motion and threw myself backwards on the bed.

"How do you even know you want to come with me? I'm not even sure where I'll go."

This was so true that every time I thought about it, panic seized me. All I knew for sure was that I couldn't stay here. Not where every corner reminded me of Ross. Not when I could see the pity in the gaze of every villager each time I spoke with them. It would be difficult to leave my father, but at least now I knew he was okay, in love, and with his hands so full with his newly acquired children that he'd hardly notice my absence.

"I doona care where ye go. It has to be better than this. Why doona ye take me to the future? There is nothing I'd like to see more."

I sighed and ran my palms over my face before rolling to bury my head into the pillow. Part of me longed to return to the twenty-first century, but it was the one thing I couldn't do. It was the only promise Ross had ever begged me to make.

"You know that I can't do that."

Olivia stared at me and I knew what she was going to say before she said it. I couldn't bear to hear her accusation one more time so I quickly held up a hand to stop her.

"Don't. Don't say that he knew about the stairwell at Cagair Castle. We didn't keep things from one another. If Ross had known, he would've told me."

Until just a few months prior, I'd believed that the only way to travel back and forth between the centuries without Ross' magic was to find another with magic, and that always seemed far too risky. But not long after Raudrich returned to The Isle of Eight Lairds, a woman showed up—a modern woman, from my own time —who'd traveled back via a magical stairwell in the castle she called home.

I'd never been so shocked to learn anything in my entire life. It was then that the two of us decided to travel to The Isle with Griffith MacChristy as our escort. We both had reasons to confront Raudrich. Sydney wished to understand why he'd so abruptly cut off contact with her, and I needed to beg him to choose another to be laird.

While I was entirely confident that Ross had no knowledge of such a stairwell, Olivia believed otherwise.

"Fine. I willna say it, but ye know deep inside that ye think it possible too. Otherwise, 'twouldna make ye so angry every time I mention it. If he dinna know there was another way for ye to get back, why would he have made ye promise to stay here?"

"He didn't want me to search for another person with magic. Time travel is dangerous, Olivia. It hurt like hell when we came back. He was only worried about my safety."

Seeing that she needed to change the subject, she sighed and moved on. "Then where will ye go? Unless ye wish to move into the cottage with Mother, yer da, Gavin, Madie, Saundra, and little Davy, ye only have tonight to decide."

"In his letter, Raudrich invited me to visit The Isle. I'm sure if he was genuine in his invitation, I could ride back with him."

"Ride back with him?"

I'd forgotten that he'd only just arrived when I bumped into him in the woods.

"He's here. He came to see Griffith settled and to reassure the people of the village once again that all is well."

Olivia grinned mischievously and wiggled her eyebrows at me. "I know why ye wish to visit The Isle."

Shaking my head, I rolled back over and scooted up until my back leaned against the headboard. "I should've never told you about what happened at the wedding."

"Told me? Ye brought me to the wedding. Ye had to tell me something when ye dinna return to our room that night."

Images of the stranger I'd found comfort with that night flooded my mind. His strong muscles, dark eyes, his lips that felt like velvet against my skin—I shuddered with need just thinking about it.

As if she could read my mind, Olivia's mouth fell open. "See? That is why ye wish to return to The Isle. Ye wish to see him again."

"Liv," before I could say another word, she placed both hands on my shoulders to stop me.

"What did ye just call me?"

Confused, I struggled to decide if she looked angry or thrilled.

"Um...I called you Liv. Did you not like it? I don't have to call you that again. It's just a nickname."

Her eyes were as wide as I'd ever seen them. "A nickname? Is this something from yer own time?"

"Not really. I'm sure there are lots of people that go by something other than their real name here."

"Aye, but they doona call them a nickname, and I've never had one." She smiled and gently shook my shoulders. "I love it. Please doona ever call me anything else."

I laughed and held out my hand to shake hers. "Agreed. Okay so, *Liv*, back to what I was saying...even if I wished to see that man again, I won't be finding him at The Isle. He was from the future, like me. I think he was just good friends with Laurel and somehow she arranged for him to come down for the wedding. I'm sure Sydney passed him through the stairwell at Cagair."

Olivia made no effort to hide her disappointment. "So ye'll never see him again?"

"Nope. I'll never see him again, and that's just fine by me."

"I doona believe ye. I saw the look in yer eye when ye stumbled back into the room after the sun was up the next day. Ye looked happy for the first time in ages."

I had been happy—happy because I'd just had some of the best sex of my life with one of the most handsome men I'd ever seen. And he'd been so kind. Perfect, really. For the night, he'd been just what I needed, but I didn't have the heart to tell sweet, innocent Olivia that sometimes what you need for a night isn't what you need for forever.

"It doesn't really matter, does it? He's in the future. I'm here in this time now. I'll never see him again. Besides, I don't even know his name."

CHAPTER 3

The Isle of Eight Lairds

"A little bit higher please, Marcus. Just three more inches, and I think I'll be able to reach it."

Holding onto both of Kate's ankles, Marcus stood on the tips of his toes so that Kate could reach the high hook with her one hand.

"You do know that I could do this with magic and it wouldn't require you treating me like a jungle gym, right?"

Grunting as she slid the picture hook over the nail installed earlier by Maddock, Kate answered him. "Yes, I know, but this is so much more fun. And it takes longer, which means you're stuck here with me for the afternoon."

Marcus never felt "stuck" when he was with Kate, but his concern for the woman standing on his shoulders did make it difficult for him to enjoy the time spent with her.

Ever since Paton—one of the eight druids sworn to protect The Isle—had hurled himself into the land of the faeries to save Kate's life, she'd been working herself to the point of exhaustion remodeling and decorating the castle. Not that the castle wasn't in need of it. Decades of being inhabited by men had taken its toll on the once glorious hallways and rooms. But Rome wasn't built in a day, and Kate seemed to be trying to renovate Murray Castle at a speed that would send her to an early grave if she didn't slow down soon.

"I can't reach any higher without levitating off the floor, which I might be able to manage if you want me to try it."

The thought of testing his magic out in such a way piqued his interest more than any other task he'd performed all morning.

"Nope. I..." He glanced up to see her reaching. "I think I've got it."

She relaxed on his shoulders as the painting slid into place.

"Okay, you can set me down now."

"Thank God. Druid or not, your bony feet hurt my shoulders."

Just before he lowered Kate to the ground, Laurel's voice boomed at them from the doorway. "What in the world are you two doing? Marcus, put her down. What if she fell and broke the one hand she has?"

Kate laughed and bent to place her palm on top of Marcus' head for support, crouched down to slip to her butt and then slowly crawled off him.

"Calm down, sis. If I broke my hand, Marcus and the other guys would heal it."

"Yes, but they wouldn't be able to do that for days—not until Raudrich returns from Allen territory. With him and Paton away... they can't risk the use of such strong magic." Laurel's words drifted as she took in Kate's expression.

Still helping her steady herself, Marcus winked reassuringly at Kate.

"He's fine, Kate. He's the power to withstand anything that old asshole of a faerie tries to do to him. The choice was his. You hold no responsibility for his actions."

"We don't know that he will be okay. We can't know that."

Laurel stepped up beside him and moved in to pull her sister close. "You're right, but we have to believe that he will be okay. It's all we can do."

Sighing, Marcus turned to leave the two sisters but was stopped by Kate's voice before he reached the doorway.

"Oh, no you don't. We're not done yet. And I don't want to talk about Paton."

Dutifully, he turned and went to lean against the new and suspiciously modern-looking kitchen island. "I really don't think I have the strength to let you stand on my shoulders for another half hour."

She dismissed him and jumped to sit on top of the island. "We're done decorating for the time being. Right now, I want to talk about you."

"About me?" Nothing she could've said would've filled him with more dread than that.

"Yes. You. We're," Kate paused and elbowed Laurel to rally her sister's support, "worried about you."

Marcus laughed and crossed his arms defensively across his chest. "You two are worried about me? You," he nodded his head toward Laurel, "have finally got your mojo back and only come out of your writing cave for a few hours a day and you," he looked at Kate, "are decorating yourself into a breakdown. You guys have to see how ironic it is that you two are worried about me."

They shrugged in unison and Marcus smiled. They never seemed to be able to see how similar they really were.

"Sure," Kate acknowledged, "we both have our problems, but that doesn't mean we can't be worried about our friend."

Laurel took a step forward and continued where Kate left off. "She's right. You had quite the active dating life back in Boston. We've been here for quite a while now, and you've had exactly no prospects and just as much action."

The center of his forehead began to throb as his brows pinched together. He would lose his mind if this became a theme around the castle. When Laurel and Kate set their minds to something, there was no deterring them.

"Ladies, I love you both, but please leave this alone. I don't need you concerning yourselves over my sex life."

"Ha." Laurel laughed. "That implies that you have one."

He jerked up from his relaxed stance and stared down at her. "You're one to talk, Laurel. Before Raudrich, how long had it been again?"

She flipped her hair over her shoulder and continued. "That is entirely beside the point. Listen. As you know, Pinkie has moved to The Isle and is—now that he's finally over his paralyzing fear of the place—working the castle grounds. As you also know, he has a daughter. I have to say, her mother must have been a stunner of a woman because you sure wouldn't think one of Pinkie's offspring would be so pretty. The girl is gorgeous, and she's rather taken with you."

Marcus had seen the girl a total of three times. On each occasion, she'd said nothing, only stared at him with wide quiet eyes before turning to run away.

"I thought she was frightened of me."

Laurel smiled and wiggled her brows. "She's not scared. She's into you. I think you should pay her a visit."

"Pay her a visit? Laurel, you've got to be joking. She's a child."

"She's not a child. She's eighteen."

He pinched the bridge of his nose as he closed his eyes and forced himself to take a deep breath. "I'm thirty. If she was a few months younger, back home, I'd be arrested for 'paying her a visit.'"

Slipping off the island, Kate stepped in between the two of them, grinning like the Cheshire cat. "But not here! Here old guys marry young girls all the time."

Laurel quickly moved to stand beside him as they stood shoulder-to-shoulder and gaped at Kate in horror.

Patiently, the two of them watched and waited for Kate to hear her own words. Slowly, she scrunched up her nose and stuck out her tongue in disgust. "Oh my gosh, I just heard it. Ugh, I didn't mean to imply you should do that. It's creepy. It's gross. Not right at all. But…in my defense, it is kind of true."

Frustrated that the two people closest to him thought that he was so desperate that it required him resorting to dating teenagers, he turned to leave the room.

Laurel quickly called after him. "Where are you going?"

"Anywhere but here. You two are crazy. Don't worry about my sex life. I'm fine. I promise."

He wasn't going to tell them his secret. He didn't want his memories of that night—of her—to belong to anyone but him.

The night of Laurel's wedding had been the best night of his life. Spent with a mysterious woman who'd been in as much need of a release as he was, he treasured each memory of that night like a precious jewel.

There was so little in his life that was now only his. The Eight shared almost everything, but that night was his special secret.

A memory he would keep only for himself.

Something he could live off for years.

CHAPTER 4

A llen Territory

For hours, Olivia talked me ragged. By the end of our conversation, I knew what I needed to do. The Isle of Eight Lairds made the most sense for so many reasons. For one, besides Allen Territory, it was literally the only place in Scotland where I actually knew anyone. I had no doubt that even if Raudrich's invitation to stay at the castle had only been out of politeness, he would at least help me find decent lodging somewhere in The Isle's main village. With any luck, he might even help me procure some sort of work to keep me busy.

Second, there were already twenty-first century women—Raudrich's wife and her sister—on The Isle. This was the most important factor because not only did it mean I had the opportunity to make friends with people who might understand me, it also meant that I could tell Raudrich the truth of where I was from and he wouldn't think I was insane or try to burn me at the stake. The only downside to telling Raudrich was that it would mean betraying my husband's secret. Ross and Raudrich had always been close, but I knew with certainty that Raudrich never knew of Ross' magic. I imagined it might be somewhat hurtful for Raudrich to now learn that his friend had kept such a huge secret from him.

Still, it was a price I was willing to pay. If I was going to start over in this time, I wanted a true fresh start. I wanted to be who I was. I wanted to speak in my own voice.

We also decided—although, I still didn't quite understand how she'd talked me into it—she was a wizard at getting her way—that perhaps it would be good for Olivia to leave home for a while. I'd agreed to speak to her mother about it first thing in the morning.

For now though, I needed to speak to Raudrich and upend everything he believed was true about me. Retracing the path I'd taken earlier, I traveled through the woods until I reached the tents Griffith and his men had set up on the edge of the village. I had a slight moment of panic when I saw the number of unmarked tents —I could just see myself creepily peeking inside a dozen of them before finding Raudrich's. But as I approached the first, I heard Raudrich's voice three tents away.

"No, Griffith, I willna join ye for more ale after dinner, and ye should abstain from it yerself, even if 'tis only for this night. Yer duties begin tomorrow."

"Which is precisely why I wish to get sloshed tonight. Ye've turned into an old man since ye got married. Ye are just like my brothers."

Raudrich laughed and gently ushered Griffith from his tent. I remained hidden in the trees until Griffith was well on his way back to the castle.

Once I could no longer hear the sounds of Griffith's rather poor whistling skills, I walked to Raudrich's tent and audibly said, "Knock, knock," to request permission to enter.

"Is that ye, Silva? Come in."

I stepped inside and smiled at the impressive set-up he had.

"Do ye mind if I speak to ye about something?"

I knew that since I was about to tell him the truth there was no real reason to use the accent, but it just felt too abrupt to drop it without explanation.

"Not at all, lass. Ye look troubled."

"No, I'm not troubled, but I do need to tell ye something."

He smiled and motioned to one of two wide and squatty logs they were using as chairs as he spoke. "Please tell me that ye intend to take me up on my offer and that ye shall come to The Isle to visit."

Part of the tension inside me relaxed. At least his invitation had been sincere. "In truth, I wanna do more than that. I wanna move there."

His eyes lit up, making me smile. "'Tis wonderful news. The women of Murray Castle will be glad to have another lass around, and we've just completed building various cottages on the castle grounds. One of them is yers if ye wish it."

I nodded in excitement. "I do wish it. But that isna what I wanted to tell ye. Raudrich." It was time to let go of the accent for good. "I'm not who you think I am. Like your wife, I'm from the twenty-first century. I, too, am American."

For a moment, I thought his brows might lift all the way off his head.

"Are ye...are ye one of Morna's lassies then?"

"Morna?" I'd never heard such a name in my life. "Who is that?"

He frowned and crossed his arms skeptically. "Morna dinna send ye to this time?"

I shook my head. "No."

"'Twas it Sydney or Gillian, then? Did ye travel through Cagair? If so, I can scarcely believe Sydney dinna tell me. We write to one another frequently."

"No. It wasn't Morna or Sydney or Gillian." I paused and took a deep breath. "Raudrich, it was Ross. Ross had magic. We...we met and married in my own time. It was only after your brother died that Ross told me the truth about who he was and we moved here."

Raudrich's suntanned skin paled making him look ill.

"Are you all right, Raudrich? Do you need me to fetch you some water? I'm sorry to tell you this. I don't know why Ross never told you. But I need to start over now, and I couldn't do that while living a lie."

Slowly, he nodded. "Ross was a druid, lass?"

I shrugged. I didn't really know what he was. I just knew what he was capable of. "Maybe. I just knew he had magic and he could travel through time."

After a brief moment of silence, the color began to return to Raudrich's face. His expression was fascinating. He wasn't angry, which was good, and surprisingly, he didn't look hurt or sad. If anything, he looked disturbed—troubled in a way that didn't make sense to me.

"Why did he insist ye use an accent, lass?"

Until Sydney arrived at the castle demanding to see Raudrich, I'd been under the impression that I was the only twenty-first century woman in seventeenth century Scotland. I'd always assumed that Ross had insisted that both my father and I assume Scottish identities to keep us safe, but as Raudrich's question had just forced me to consider, I now wasn't so sure.

When I didn't answer him right away, Raudrich shook his head, and his teeth ground together enough to make his jawbone bulge. "To make certain that none here knew of his magic."

I nodded. It was the only thing that made sense. "I suppose so. Look, I understand if you don't want me to come to The Isle. I can find somewhere else to live."

"Lass." He released the tension in his jaw and turned sympathetic eyes on me. "O'course ye should come to The Isle if ye wish it. Ross was my friend, but ye are, as well. I must ask ye though, why would ye wish to start over here? Do ye not wish to go back to yer own time?"

"Right after Ross died that was all I wanted to do, but my father is here. Even though I don't want to live here in Allen territory, I don't wish to be so far away from him either. Besides, I promised Ross before he died that I would never go back."

Raudrich appeared genuinely concerned. "Why would ye promise him that?"

"He asked me to."

The muscle in Raudrich's jaw bulged out again. "Why would he do that?"

"He worried that I would try to find someone else with magic that could send me back, and he wouldn't have wanted me to place such trust in someone. Not when the travel is so difficult and painful."

"'Tis not difficult or painful at all through Cagair. He should have told ye to travel through there if ye wished it."

"He might have had he known about it."

Raudrich sighed and stood. "Lass, he did know of the portal at Cagair Castle. I told Ross many stories of Sydney's travels through the portal."

It took a moment for Raudrich's words to sink in. As they did, I began to shake.

Ross had lied through omission. Lied about something that could drastically change my life.

"So you don't believe that he told me to stay here because he was worried about my safety?"

"Before ye walked in this tent, I could have told ye why I believe Ross did a great many things, but now I feel I doona know him at all."

"What do you mean?" I stood to try and better gauge his expression.

"Nothing, lass. 'Tis only the knowledge that Ross held magic comes as quite a shock. Ye are welcome to join us at The Isle. Indeed, I insist that ye do just that."

I could sense that he was ready for me to leave, and I was more than eager to do so.

My husband was a liar. Learning that he'd known about Cagair and kept it from me felt as if my every memory of him was shattered somehow, distorted, different, poisoned in a way that I wasn't sure I could ever get back. I wished I'd never said anything to Raudrich.

And worse, Raudrich clearly knew more about my husband than he was letting on.

Why was my father the only man in my life that believed I could handle the truth?

CHAPTER 5

*A*llen Castle had a storeroom filled with ale and wine collected for years from traveling merchants. Angry and heartbroken, I visited said storeroom on my way back to the master bedchamber of the castle.

Intending to drown my sorrows, I stepped inside to find Olivia still sprawled out on the bed reading.

Gripping a container of wine in each hand, I stepped inside, and in a split-second decision decided to corrupt my younger sister.

"Olivia, you're twenty years old. Have you ever been drunk?"

Slowly, like I'm-sure-I-didn't-just-hear-you-right slowly, she closed her book and rose from the bed.

Suspiciously, she eyed what I held in my hands.

"No, I canna say that I have. Silva, are ye all right?"

I shook my head, and set both of the oddly shaped containers down on the small table before reaching for the two empty mugs.

"Nope, Liv. I am not all right. You were right. Ross knew about Cagair. He knew and he didn't tell me. If he knew, why would he make me promise to stay here, Liv? Why wouldn't he want me to return to my old life if that's what I wanted? It has me questioning everything."

As slowly as she'd closed her book, she stood and stared at me a long moment before saying anything. When she did speak, she did so while walking toward me with both arms extended.

"Ach, Silva. Please come and give me a hug."

I wasn't exactly in the hugging mood, but I was rarely able to deny Olivia anything. Reluctantly, I moved to wrap my arms around her. The moment I did so, she hugged me tight and soothingly patted the back of my hair.

"I am sorry that he lied to ye. It brings me no pleasure to know that I was right, but this is yer last night in this castle and none of yer belongings are readied for travel. Ye doona have time to question everything this night. For now, why doona ye put Ross out of yer mind? If ye wish to get dizzy with ale, we shall do so, but we must begin packing ye while we drink. On the road, once we are away from here, ye can question as much as ye wish to."

Sometimes, Olivia would say something that made me realize that I didn't give her enough credit. She was wiser than she looked and perhaps not as naive as I perceived her to be.

"You're pretty smart, you know."

She laughed and pulled away. "Would ye tell that to my mother when ye speak to her tomorrow?"

"I will. Now are you ready for your first hangover?"

"What is that?

I patted her on the shoulder gently.

"Oh sweetheart, you'll see soon enough."

The two of us had no problem finishing off the wine I'd smuggled from the castle storeroom, and together we spent the night laughing and packing up a roomful of memories that I no longer knew how to feel about.

CHAPTER 6

The Isle of Eight Lairds

"Marcus, lad, I was hoping ye would come tonight. The last two nights with Nicol have been a misery. In truth, I am glad to be free of him."

The garden was Marcus' favorite place in the castle, and its permanent resident was quite possibly Marcus' favorite human—if she could be called that—of all time.

While most of The Eight rotated between castle duties, Marcus' magic seemed to be just what the garden needed; therefore, he'd been named its permanent caretaker. That suited him just fine. It meant that the garden was his sanctuary, a place that—since she'd already completed her work there—Kate's decorating couldn't even touch. While most of the time he worked in the garden during the day, on the nights when Nicol chose not to spend the evening with his ghostly wife in the garden, Marcus would return in the evening to visit with Freya.

His conversations with her always brought him joy, but like

Kate, Freya was another subject of worry in his life. For the first many months after Marcus arrived on The Isle with Laurel, Freya's essence was as visible to the human eye as human flesh, but over the past weeks—since Paton's imprisonment with the fae—she appeared more translucent, as if she were disappearing before their very eyes.

Marcus suspected this had more than a little to do with Nicol's increasingly frequent absences from the garden. If Nicol's observational skills were even half that of Marcus', Freya's husband had to be wondering the same thing—was Freya nearing a time when she would leave them for good?

"Of course I would come. I already told you—on nights when Nicol is kept away, I'm your man. I'll be here to visit for as long as you like."

She patted the stone bench where they had all of their conversations and Marcus gladly joined her.

"Marcus, ye needn't keep pretending as if important matters keep Nicol away. I know why he doesna come to see me as he once did."

"You do?" The last thing Marcus wished to do was put a worry in Freya's mind that wasn't already there.

"Aye. The recent couplings around the castle—Raudrich and Laurel, Maddock and Kate, even Ludo has been courting a lass in the village—they've made it more difficult for Nicol to be so separated from me."

"I don't understand what you mean."

Marcus did indeed have some idea what Freya might mean, but he knew enough about women to know better than to say something that might hurt her. If she was thinking it, she should be the one to say it aloud—not him.

"Ye must know. Before, when all of ye lads were more lonesome than him, 'twas easy to make peace with the truth that we couldna ever truly be together again. That only in this way, through our conversations, through our minds, could we show each other love.

Now that carnal love has found its way back inside the castle, he sees what he misses. I doona blame him. It makes me miss it more too."

Marcus couldn't imagine living in Freya's frozen state. Forever untouchable, forever ageless, forever cursed to appear only at night in a garden separated from the man she loved most in the world.

He said nothing. He didn't need to. He could sense that Freya wasn't finished.

"Everything that has happened is good. Love desperately needed to return to this place. But it means that both Nicol and I must make peace with change, and change isna always easy. He must learn to forgive himself for wandering, and I must learn to make peace with my death once again."

"Wander?" Marcus nearly choked on his own spit. "Nicol would never stray, Freya. He loves you."

She smiled, and the look in Freya's eyes made him feel like an ignorant child.

"Aye, o'course he loves me, but I am dead, Marcus. In every way that matters, I am dead. 'Tis not truly wandering, but if ye doona believe that on nights when Nicol doesna come here that he is with another, then ye are a fool. He is. I can see it in his eyes when he returns. And that is as it should be. 'Twill make it easier on him when Machara is defeated and I am gone, if he has someone else."

Freya sighed, and in the brief silence, Marcus tried to grapple with the news Freya had just shared with him. None of the other members of The Eight would ever suspect this. They all knew how much of Nicol's heart Freya occupied.

"Doona look so distraught, lad. I am not angry with him. I only wish 'twas easier for me to let go of my humanity. I know that I am dead, but in truth, in the time before things began to change here, I allowed myself to live in the same blissful ignorance as Nicol. 'Twas simpler to make peace with my death when there was no threat of Machara's defeat. And 'twas much easier to miss the touch of my husband when I wasna so constantly reminded of how marvelous physical love is.

"I know that I am fading. Machara and I are tied. When Brachan broke his bond to her, it shattered something inside Machara she dinna know she had. She's retreated in a way she has never done before. The women are doing what they were always meant to. It willna be long before Machara is gone. With her death, so I shall go. In truth I may pass even before her death. I can sense my tie to her breaking."

Marcus had always known this about Freya. They all knew that it was Machara's power that sustained Freya's half-alive state, but he'd never truly allowed it to sink in that once Machara was defeated—let alone possibly before—that Freya would leave them and experience her true and final death.

It wasn't acceptable. Freya was too good, and Nicol loved her too much.

He loved her too much.

If there was a way to save her, he would find it.

"I'm sorry, Freya." His mind made up, Marcus quickly made his excuses. "There's something I've forgotten that I must take care of immediately."

For as long as it took to find an answer, the libraries of Murray Castle would be his constant companion.

llen Territory

Olivia—damn her—looked no worse for wear upon waking the next morning. In fact, I was half-convinced that she'd only pretended to drink last night. By the time I woke, she was already sitting in the corner of the room munching on some breakfast she'd taken from the kitchen, reading one of her beloved books.

I allowed myself to get ready for the day rather slowly. My head ached from too much wine, and the last thing I needed was to look how I felt, while trying to convince Leanna to entrust her daughter to me for the foreseeable future.

I took special time to pin my hair up in a way that made me look older and—I hoped—more responsible. Olivia seemed to understand precisely what I was doing.

"Ye should wear yer gray dress. It covers more of ye. Makes ye look like a ma."

"What does that mean – 'like a ma'?"

"'Tis boring, Silva. The cut of that dress went out of style ages ago."

I snorted and reached for the plain, gray dress. It seemed so strange that anything from this time could be considered "out of style," then again, change was the one constant throughout all of time. Even in the seventeenth century, there would be things considered no longer fashionable.

"Ye must convince her, Silva, for I swear to ye, I'm coming with ye either way. I'd rather things not be out of sorts with my mother."

Taking one last glance at myself in the long looking glass Ross had acquired at my pestering, I nodded and made my way toward the door.

"I'll do my best. Wish me luck."

She called after me as I left. "Ye shall need it."

*E*ntering Dad and Leanna's house always made me laugh. I couldn't remember my father ever being very "fatherly." He was a great dad, but from the time I was old enough to talk, it had always felt more like he was my best friend than anything else. He certainly never reminded me of the dads my best friends had growing up.

Our home had been a calm and orderly place. Rather than dolls or dress-up, we played puzzle games and did things like repair his old boat. While he was crazy about me, kids in general had never really been Dad's cup of tea. The fact that he was now surrounded by them every second of every day and loved it was proof of how funny life can be.

"Silva." He greeted me with a smile as I stepped inside. They all sat around the table eating breakfast. He held little Davy in his lap while the toddler gnawed on a piece of bread. "Come and join us."

"I don't need anything to eat, but I'll come and sit with you guys until you're done. Here." I extended my arms to Davy and he reached toward me with his spare hand—his other was still occupied by the large piece of bread he was holding. "I'll hold Davy so you can finish eating."

To Davy more than any of the other children, my dad would always be his. Leanna's first husband had passed away only weeks into her pregnancy with Davy, and Leanna and my Dad met when the child was only two months old.

Leanna, while undoubtedly in a state of constant exhaustion, hid it insanely well. She always managed to look effortlessly perfect. It was the only thing about her that made it difficult for me to like her. If I'd pushed out seven children by the age of thirty-four, especially in this century, I was quite certain that my tits would be down to my knees and every hair on my head would be as gray as the sky on a rainy day in Scotland.

"Did ye and Olivia manage to pack all yer things away?"

"We did." I could see no sense in delaying the inevitable. "Leanna, when you get a chance, do you think the two of us could have a chat?"

Dad, seemingly sensing the importance in my voice, quickly stood and began rounding up the other children.

"Gavin, gather your and Madie's food. I'll get Saundra's and Davy's. It's a warm enough morning. Let's go and enjoy it in the grass out back."

Eager for any excuse to be outdoors, the children quickly scattered, and Dad winked at me as the group exited.

"Ye have made me anxious, Silva. What is it?"

I stood and moved two chairs closer to her. "It is about Olivia."

"Olivia? Is she in trouble? Ye know, I havena seen her since Thursday. The lass flits around here and there like a firefly. She is restless. She needs to settle down—'twould settle her soul a bit."

Or crush it, I thought. Olivia was far too young to do any such thing. She knew too little about the world—too little about herself to attach herself to any place, or person.

"Leanna, I know I am not Olivia's mother, but that is the last thing she needs. I'm leaving here now that Griffith is taking over my duties. I plan to settle on The Isle of Eight Lairds. Olivia wishes to come with me, and I really think you should let her go."

Leanna looked horrified. "Why would ye leave here? Yer family is here. Yer da, me, the children. And why would ye ever think Olivia should leave here? Ye must know I wouldna allow it."

"I can't stay here. Since Ross passed away, I can't seem to catch my breath here. There are too many memories, too many reminders of him everywhere."

She lifted one brow and I knew precisely what she was thinking, although she said nothing. She, too, had lost a husband. She, too, still lived in the home they'd made together. She, too, had memories of him haunting her every corner.

"I could stay here like you, Leanna, but I don't want to, and that's my choice to make. And why, precisely, would you not allow Olivia to leave here if she wishes it? Olivia is smart and adventurous. She needs to figure out who she is in the world away from here. In this village, everyone will always see her as a child."

"She is not a child. By the time I was her age, I'd been married for eight years and birthed three bairns. God rest little Rabbie's soul."

"Exactly, Leanna. Olivia is not a child. The decision shouldn't be yours to make. If your own life had turned out differently, if you'd had the opportunity to leave here and explore other places for a while, wouldn't you have taken it?"

She stared at me for a long moment and slowly, I began to hope. Something in her eyes seemed to be shifting. Leanna's life had been filled with few choices, and I could see that she could see sense in allowing her daughter to have more than she ever did.

"O'course I would have. Ye must know 'tisna customary. Until Olivia is wed, she should be here in our home. The only thing that makes it acceptable for ye to live alone is that ye are already a widow."

I had to strain to keep from rolling my eyes. Customary anything could shove it.

"I know. Does that mean you'll allow her to come with me?"

She sighed and rested her chin in the palm of her hand as she leaned into the table. "Aye, but, Silva, ye are taking all responsibility for her, do ye understand? If anything should happen to her, it shall be ye I will blame for it."

That seemed rather harsh to me. She had to know better than anyone that Olivia pretty much always did exactly as she pleased, but I knew if I said anything of the sort that Leanna would revoke her permission.

"I understand. Everything will be fine."

"It better be. Olivia is everything I never got to be. I couldna ever go on without her."

"We've never been more than a few miles apart from one another. I'm going to miss you more than I can say."

Full-on blubbering, Dad pulled me into a giant, bone-crushing hug as my own tears wet the front of his shirt.

"I know. But you—"

He interrupted me before I could finish. "Of course I understand. There's nothing for you here. Though I do wish you would consider going back home. Now that you know of Cagair, you could still come back and visit."

I started to speak, but he held up a hand to stop me.

"I know what you promised him, but sweetheart, he's gone. And to me—and I know I'm just your defensive old man—the fact that he never told you about Cagair makes his request null and void."

Every time I thought about Ross' lie, my insides turned cold and my stomach flipped over. It made Ross feel like a stranger to me.

Clinging to him for support, I continued to cry into his chest.

"I'm so angry with him, Dad. Angry for lying, and mostly angry that he brought me here only to die so soon after. He upended my whole life. The cost was worth it to be with him, but without him, it all seems too high."

Dad reached for my hand and gently spun the ring I still wore on my left ring finger.

"You've got to let him go. All this anger, all this hurt—leaving here will solve nothing for you unless you've placed all that in the past. However you need to do it, make peace with him before you leave. It's time for you to say goodbye."

I'd never been up to the top of the mountain that sat as the backdrop to Allen Territory. It was a pilgrimage many from the village often made, but it had always been a sacred place for Ross, and I'd never felt the need to intrude.

Now, however, it felt necessary that I make the trip. Something there had broken him. He'd been whole when he left me that morning, and by the time he returned from the mountain that night, he was already halfway gone. It was there—at the place where he began to leave me—that I would bid him one final farewell.

The trek was an easy one, the path well-worn from regular use. It wound and weaved its way up easily. The top of the mountain was beautiful.

A small river stream cut the flat top of the mountain in half. The grass was abundantly green on either side and the water's source lay within a wide-mouthed cave, all bubbling up from a circular well that must have gone all the way down to the base of the mountain.

"Ross," I said his name softly, falling to my knees beside the well. I often spoke out loud to him, but I knew he never heard me. Perhaps here, he would. "I'm so angry with you. Angry that you died, angry that you brought me here, angry that you made me make a promise based on a lie." I was sobbing now, and for the first time in months, I didn't try to stop the stream of tears. "And I'm angry that you were so powerful in life and so damned useless in death. How could a man that could travel through time, that could do just about anything with the flick of his wrist, not at least let me feel him? How could you be so powerful in life and not give me the least little sign in death that you are still around in some way?"

I don't know what I expected. A big gust of wind, a voice, all I knew was that something deep inside me really did believe that here in this place so tangibly filled with magic, that *something* would happen.

Nothing did.

"Ross," I was screaming at him now, my hands shaking as I pulled my wedding band from my finger. "If you're here, I need you to show me. If not, I'm letting you go and with it any promises that we made."

Still, there was nothing.

Blinded by grief, anger, and embarrassment at my own stupidity, I flung my ring into the well and watched helplessly as it sunk to God only knew where.

I sobbed for hours, until all of my tears ran dry.

By the time I rose from the ground at dusk, I was empty, but to my agony, I still felt no more free of him.

CHAPTER 8

The Isle of Eight Lairds

Covered in soil up to his elbows, Marcus worked the garden's newest flowers into place. The once open-air garden was no longer controlled by Scotland's often intemperate weather. He enjoyed taking full advantage of being able to find and plant whatever would be the most beautiful, only employing the use of magic when absolutely necessary. He enjoyed the satisfaction of seeing things bloom from hard work and care alone.

The sound of hooves and chatter stirred him from his work. Raudrich's voice he recognized, but it surprised him to hear other voices with him. Had he brought guests back from Allen Territory?

Rinsing his arms in the small garden well, he stepped outside to greet whoever was coming. It was a short walk from the garden entrance to the stables. As Raudrich rode in front of the two horses behind him, Marcus called out to his friend.

"Did you pick up stragglers on your way home?"

He asked the question in jest, expecting to see two men ride up beside him. Instead, two ladies emerged—one of them he'd never seen before, but the other he would've recognized anywhere. It was the woman from the wedding—the stranger he dreamed about with shocking regularity.

The woman he'd been certain he would never see again.

Every muscle in his body tensed as he watched recognition wash over the woman's face. She looked as surprised as he felt.

"Ach, ye could say that. This..." Raudrich paused for just a moment to gesture to the woman on his left, and Marcus prepared himself to hear her name for the first time. "...is Silva, the lass who took over my duties in Allen Territory. I just relieved her of said duties, and she has come to the castle to live with us for the time being. And this..."

Marcus knew it was unkind, but he was no longer listening to Raudrich's introduction of the woman to his right. His mind spun with what Raudrich had just revealed to him. The woman he'd slept with the night of Laurel's wedding was Silva—the widow Raudrich so often spoke of with reverence for the strength she showed through her grief?

He'd bedded a woman in mourning.

It made him feel rotten. Even though there was no way for him to know about the woman's grief—not when they'd both agreed to cast their identities aside for the night—he still couldn't help but feel like he'd somehow done something untoward to her. Taking advantage in a way he never would have done had he known.

"Marcus?" Raudrich's concerned voice pulled him from his thoughts.

"Do ye wish to say hello to the lassies or just stare at them?"

He cleared his throat and recovered as best he could. "Of course I do. Welcome to you both." He moved over to the woman on Raudrich's right and reached for her hand so that he could kiss her knuckles.

"I'm so sorry. Can you tell me your name again?"

The girl—he didn't imagine she was much older than Pinkie's daughter— smiled as his lips brushed her fingers.

"Aye, I'm Olivia, but please call me Liv. Everyone does."

Silva snorted, and it was the first time he'd heard her so much as breathe since she lay eyes on him.

"Everyone calls ye that now, do they?"

Marcus watched as Liv pulled her brows together in confusion and turned toward Silva's voice.

"Well, I'd like them to, aye?"

Giving her fingers a gentle squeeze, he released his grip on her hand.

"Liv it is then. Welcome to the castle. It's really not too bad once you get used to it."

Hoping that his nerves wouldn't get the best of him, he slowly walked toward Silva and reached for her hand. "It's wonderful to see you again." He paused, and with great intention, said her name for the first time. "Silva."

He could hear Raudrich dismount behind him as his friend stated the obvious question. "Ye two know each other?"

There was a plea in Silva's eyes that made his heart hurt. Silently, she begged him to say nothing, and it shocked him to think that she would ever believe he would speak of something so private so freely.

Giving her a nod so small that no one else would notice, he kissed her hand and let it drop back to her lap.

"She was at your wedding, remember? We met then."

"We were both at the wedding."

Ashamed that he had no recollection of the girl, Marcus faced Liv to apologize.

"Right you are. I thought you looked familiar, although I don't think we had a chance to say hello to each other that night."

"We dinna. 'Tis lovely to meet ye now though."

"Agreed."

He reached for Raudrich's horse while the women dismounted.

"I can see the horses to the stables, if you want to see them settled, Raudrich?"

Raudrich walked over and placed a firm hand on his shoulder before speaking lowly in his ear. "Aye, thank ye. I'll take them each to their own cabin and have Henry fetch them hot water for baths. Once the horses are settled, please round up everyone else in the castle. We must all discuss our new guests before dinner."

CHAPTER 9

*T*he walk from the front of the castle to the amazingly beautiful cabins in the back stretched on for an eternity. Every limb, toe, and finger trembled in response to the shock of seeing my one-night-only lover standing there waiting to greet us when we arrived. Whether Raudrich could sense how shaken I was, I couldn't say, but Olivia was acutely aware of how pale I'd gone.

"Do ye need me to hold ye up, Silva? Ye look as if ye might fall down."

Looping her arm through mine, she slowed me down a step so that the distance between Raudrich and us grew just a little.

"I feel as if I might. Just don't ask me anything until we are safely inside, okay? I'll explain what's going on in a minute."

When we arrived at the fourth cabin along a curved stone path of ten such cabins, Raudrich lifted the latch and held the door open for us so we could step inside.

"This one here shall be yers, Silva. There are candles all around so that when lit, the room is quite bright. One of us will come by each night to see them lit for ye. Henry shall be along shortly with hot water so ye may take a bath and rest. I'll return shortly with yer trunks. I'll set them outside so as not to disturb ye. If there is anything ye may need, please let one of us know. We eat at dusk in the main dining hall. Everyone will look forward to meeting you then."

Giving me a gentle smile, he faced Olivia. "Yer cabin is the one immediately to the right. They are twins of each other. Would ye like me to escort ye there?"

Olivia's entire face lit with glee. "Ye mean I get my own cabin? I've never had so much as a trunk to meself before."

Raudrich nodded, his smile wide. I could see he was pleased to make her so happy. "Aye, all yers. Henry is fetching water for ye as well."

Olivia took one giant step toward him and threw her arms around his middle. "Thank ye. Thank ye. Thank ye. I shall never be able to thank ye enough."

Laughing, Raudrich gently patted Olivia's back with one of his giant hands. "There is no need to thank me, lass. We all only wish that ye enjoy yer time here. Do ye wish me to walk ye over?"

"No, thank ye. I'll stay here with Silva for a moment."

Giving us each a nod, he turned to leave, but paused in the doorway as he looked back over his shoulder. "Silva, lass, why did ye pretend to be Scottish with Marcus before? I thought ye wished to start over here."

Letting out a shaky breath, I gripped the edge of the most decadent copper tub I'd ever seen as I lied through my teeth.

"Did I? I didn't even realize. Sorry, it's just a habit. I'll try not to do it again."

"'Tis not my concern how ye speak, lass. I only wanted to make sure that ye still wished to live honestly here. If ye doona, I can keep yer secret."

"No. I'm ready to be me." It was the only thing I was sure of.

"Verra well. I'll see ye both in a while."

Olivia waited all of three seconds after Raudrich was gone

before ushering me over to the bed and gently pushing me so that I would sit on its edge.

"Breathe, Silva. Ye must breathe. I wouldna know what to do if ye fainted."

"I'm not going to faint. I'm just rattled."

"Why? I thought Marcus seemed…" She trailed off as she read my expression. "Ohhh…he's the man from the wedding, aye?"

"Yes."

Reaching for a chair just to her right, Olivia pulled it toward her and sat across from me as she gathered my hands up in hers. "I thought ye said he was from yer time? That he was just a friend of Laurel's that she brought back for the wedding?"

"He is from my time. Couldn't you tell?"

Olivia pulled away and leaned back in the chair to cross her arms. "He talks as ye do, but how can he be from yer time? He's one of The Eight, aye? A druid?"

I shrugged. "He must be—although, I didn't have the slightest idea at the wedding. We told each other virtually nothing about ourselves. I only assumed that he was brought back for the wedding because he was so obviously from my time. It never occurred to me that he lived here, let alone that he was one of The Eight."

Olivia smiled cautiously. "'Tis a bonny surprise, aye? Ye enjoyed yer time with him."

I'd enjoyed my time with him immensely, but I knew how much healing I still needed to do—healing that would be much more difficult with such an enticing distraction hanging around the castle.

"I did, but my life is beyond complicated right now."

Exhaustion beyond anything I'd ever experienced before washed over me in a wave that made it impossible for me to stay upright. Allowing myself to relax, I crawled onto the bed and into the fetal position.

"If you want to go to dinner, you're welcome to, but I'm not leaving this bed until morning. I just need some time to decompress."

I allowed my eyes to close, but something inside me suspected my rest would be short-lived.

CHAPTER 10

*E*veryone sat gathered around the castle's main dining table hours before supper, each of them awaiting Raudrich's arrival so that he would tell them whatever he needed to about their new guests.

"Do you know what this is about? You said you saw them when they arrived," Laurel whispered in his ear, and Marcus couldn't help but laugh that Raudrich's wife thought he might know more about this than her.

"No, I have no idea. I only interacted with them for a few minutes."

"I've only been around Silva a few times. Once when she came here with Sydney to ask Raudrich to find someone else to run Allen Territory, and I believe I spoke to her for a moment at the wedding. I always thought she seemed rather nice. I wonder what's going on."

Nodding toward the doorway as Raudrich entered, both he and Laurel settled back in their seats with the rest of them to await Raudrich's explanation.

Nicol stood from his place of honor at the end of the table and gently demanded an explanation. "Raudrich, lad, what is this about? Ye've got us all worried ye are having us harbor a murderer."

61

"Ye can sit down, Nicol. 'Tis nothing as terrible as that. I only thought it best that everyone here understand the situation before we welcome Silva and Olivia into our lives. I doona believe she is in a place where she will feel like telling ye all the same tale over and over."

"Verra well." Nicol resumed his seat. "Whatever 'tis, tell us."

"I know that none of ye knew him, but I grew up with Silva's late husband. Until the time he found work in another territory and I came here, he was my best mate and closest confidant. While there were a great many years that we dinna see each other, I still always believed that I knew him. I dinna know him at all." Sighing, Raudrich continued.

"Silva isna precisely who she has always presented herself to be, though that is no fault of her own. Ye see, Ross had magic, and, like our friend Morna, could travel through time. It seems he found Silva in the same time as several who sit at this table. They fell in love, he married her, and he brought her back here, all while convincing her of the importance of keeping the truth about herself a secret."

Silva was modern? Marcus' mind spun as he tried to search for any clue to such truth from their night together. He could find none.

Brachan, the newest member of The Eight, spoke from the other side of the table. "And ye dinna know this? Ye couldna sense the magic within him?"

Raudrich's eyes closed as he shook his head. "No, which means Ross' abilities with magic far outweigh any of our own. He was able to conceal it not only from me, but from everyone who knew him."

Ludo leaned forward, his eyes grim. "Raudrich, how did Ross die?"

Marcus could all but hear Raudrich's teeth grind together, and as he observed the stress on his friend's face, realization sunk in.

Those with magic didn't die easily. In truth, he knew of only three ways. Another with magic could kill them, they could choose through violent means to kill themselves, or, when old age was upon them and their soul was ready to leave, they could gently and easily choose to pass.

"A rapid illness of the chest, or so Silva believes."

"Were ye not there at the time of Ross' supposed death?" Ludo's suspicions had quickly taken him to what they were all beginning to wonder.

"No. I was away the day he died. I know what ye mean to suggest, Ludo, and I'm afraid I believe as ye do. Ross was too young, and he wanted too much, to let himself pass at such an age. I believe he lives."

The very thought that anyone would put their spouse through such unnecessary grief by faking their own death enraged Marcus. If he ever crossed paths with the loathsome creature, he'd break his neck. He spoke for the first time since Raudrich began. "Does Silva suspect this, as well?"

"No, and I doona wish for any of ye to say a word to her of this."

"Raudrich, she deserves to know."

"Aye, she does, but I should be the one to tell her. I dinna know how to when she first told me the truth. I still doona truly know how. I will tell her the truth, but there is no rush in it. If he wished to leave in such a way, I doona think he shall be coming back for her."

"What a moronic fool."

Every head at the table turned to stare at him.

Marcus shrugged. "What? Only a total prick would treat anyone that way."

Raudrich nodded in agreement. "Aye, I'm so angry with him that if indeed he does live, I shall kill him all over again, but Silva must be our main concern. She wishes for nothing more than to start anew here. We must allow her the time and space to do just that."

Laurel scooted up closer to the table beside him. "Why wouldn't she return to the future? I mean, we've..." She paused and motioned to Marcus, Kate, her mother, and Marcus' dad, David before continuing. "We've all grown accustomed to living in this time, but I think I can easily speak for all of us when I say that if the people we loved weren't here, we'd go back to regular toilet paper and central heating and air in a heartbeat."

Marcus, along with the rest of the castle's twenty-first century residents, nodded in agreement.

Raudrich's lips hardly moved as he answered and his anger was evident in his tone. "He made her promise to never go back."

"What sort of a bullshit promise is that?" Marcus glanced over to see Kate looking riled up three seats down from him. "I mean seriously, you don't get to force anyone into making any sort of deathbed promise when you're faking your own death."

"She doesna know he faked anything, lass, and for now, she canna know."

"But why would he make her promise that?"

Marcus couldn't see the sense in it. If Ross didn't want to be with her, why did he care where or when she chose to live?

"Canna ye see? He left her here and fled back to the twenty-first century so he couldna ever be found."

---

*H*is nerves leading up to dinner were for naught— neither Silva nor Olivia joined them. It didn't surprise him. The journey from just about anywhere to The Isle was an exhausting one, and shock always had a way of making people tired.

Exhausted or not, Marcus suspected that both of the women would be hungry.

"Raudrich," Marcus called out to him as everyone began to scatter for the evening.

"Aye?"

"Which cabins did you place Silva and Olivia in? I thought I might bring them each some food since they didn't come down to eat."

"We've had the same idea. I just asked Brachan to see that each lass received a decent meal. I believe he's down in the kitchen gathering it all up."

Eager to catch Brachan before he left, he nodded and turned to jog toward the kitchen. "Okay, I'll find him."

Marcus was pleased with his luck. Brachan would be much easier to deal with than any of the other members of The Eight. He and the once half-fae son of Nicol and Machara were the newest members of The Eight by far and as such held the shared experience of learning how things worked around the castle at the same time.

Brachan was also far less likely to pry every last detail out of him. The man was a deep thinker who only spoke when he truly had something to say.

"Do you mind if I steal that job from you?"

Brachan didn't lift his head at the sound of Marcus' voice right away, and Marcus watched on patiently as his ever-particular friend finished wrapping up a loaf of bread in a linen cloth. When he finished, Brachan looked up to answer him.

"O'course not, though surely ye have enough work to tend to without relieving me of mine. Are ye certain?"

Marcus gave Brachan a quick nod as he reached for the impeccably prepared baskets. "Yes, I am, although I'll be sure to give you credit for the work. I visited with Silva at the wedding for a while. I thought it might be nice for her to see a familiar face."

With the respect Marcus had known Brachan would give him, he simply smiled and stepped away from the table. "Verra well. I shall leave ye to it, then."

Silva would appreciate the gesture, but Marcus knew his

reasons for bringing food weren't entirely selfless. Speaking of their night together was inevitable now that Silva planned to live at the castle. Better to do it now before the others overwhelmed her with questions and efforts to make her feel at home.

Once she was introduced to all the others, he'd never be able to find a moment alone with her.

CHAPTER 11

J'm not sure why I ever believed that my emotional exhaustion would actually make me sleep. Nothing in my history indicated that might happen. Even during the worst periods of grief following Ross' death—when everyone said that grief was exhausting and I should sleep as much as I could—sleep never found me. Insomnia always seemed to be the way my body responded to just about any sort of stress.

When there was a knock on the door to my cabin several hours after Olivia left, I was more than ready for her company once again.

"Come in, Liv. I'm sorry I dismissed you so rudely before. I just…" I paused as the door opened and the tall, broad frame of the man I'd fantasized about so many times since Raudrich and Laurel's wedding appeared in the partially open doorway.

He held a basket out toward me as he spoke. "Sorry to disappoint you. I'm not Liv. I just thought that you might be hungry after traveling all day. I don't even have to come inside if you don't want me to. I can just set this down right here." He leaned forward to set the basket on the floor and I hurriedly jumped up from the bed to stop him.

Despite the shock of finding him at the castle, the truth was, I was happy to see him. Marcus—even though I'd only learned his name a few hours ago—was the one person, outside of Olivia or my dad, since Ross' death that I'd been able to truly relax around.

"No, that's all right. Please, come in. I'm sorry I was so strange earlier. It was…"

He smiled as he interrupted me, and the image of him in candlelight as he stepped fully inside the room flooded my mind with memories of our night spent together.

"A shock. Yes, I know. For me too. Do you mind if I stay for a bit? If it makes you uncomfortable to eat alone, I'll eat for a second time. I'm afraid I have a bottomless stomach."

He looked like all he ever ate was protein and vegetables, and I couldn't help but wonder if he'd always been so spectacularly shaped or if life in the seventeenth century with its limited junk food and hard ways had molded him into what he was today.

I snorted and quickly ran my hands over the top of my hair to smooth it as he turned his back to set the basket on the circular table near the doorway.

"It doesn't look like anything you eat is sticking with you."

He laughed as his dark eyes glanced at me over his shoulder and he nodded his head toward the table so I would join him. "I have my father to thank for that. The man is sixty-two years old and he has the body of someone two decades younger."

"It's the same way with my dad. Everyone has a difficult time believing he's old enough to be my father when I introduce him. Granted, he was very young when I was born, but he still has aged remarkably well."

Marcus nodded and pulled out one of the chairs around the table to take a seat.

I joined him and didn't hesitate to begin to rifle through the variety of goodies he'd brought me.

"You really didn't have to go to all of this trouble. We could've waited until morning. Do you mind if I pop over and give some of this to Olivia before we settle in for the inevitable chat I know that we both know we need to have?"

He reached for some bread and swallowed a small bite before he spoke. "Already done. I stopped at her cottage on my way here."

Of course he had. Even though I knew his motive for bringing the food was to discuss things now so we could avoid the awkwardness of hashing things out later, only someone truly thoughtless would have brought only one traveler food while neglecting the other, and I knew Marcus wasn't that.

"Oh. Good." Embarrassed that I'd assumed he hadn't thought of Olivia, I began to look through the basket once more, pretending I hadn't already seen every single thing that was inside.

"Listen." He hesitated and I glanced up from the food. I was relieved that he was going to delve into it first. "Please don't think that I plan on making this a big deal. I don't. I know that you want to start over here, and I will do everything I can to help you do that. I just know that if we are going to be living in such close quarters, it might be best to address what happened between us now and get any of the awkwardness out of the way early on."

"Agreed."

He continued. "Silva—the name suits you, by the way. I feel as if I owe you an apology. Had I known…"

I cringed as I anticipated his next words and I reached out to place my hand on his arm to stop him. God, his skin was soft.

"Please don't say you wouldn't have done it. I didn't tell you I was a widow because I wanted you to do it. I regret nothing about that night, and it would take some of the joy out of it if I thought you did."

He looked relieved, and although I didn't want to, I pulled my hand away from him. "I don't regret it. Not at all. But…" He bit at his lower lip as if he wasn't sure if he should finish his sentence, but before I could say anything to encourage him, he continued. "I'd be lying if I said I would've done it had I known. I probably wouldn't have. It would've seemed like I was taking advantage of your grief somehow, and that's the last thing I would ever want to do."

He must've seen my face fall just a bit, for he quickly continued.

"But...that doesn't mean I wouldn't have wanted to. I would have. And I respect your decision not to tell me. You owed me nothing that night. I was a stranger."

I smiled and reached for a wedge of cheese inside the basket. "You still are."

He leaned back in the chair and crossed his arms which caused his muscles to strain against his shirt. I was fairly positive he did it just so I would look at them. "True."

He patiently watched me as I continued to eat and I admired that the silence didn't seem to make him uncomfortable.

"Marcus?"

He smiled and lifted his brows. "That's the first time you've said my name. You looked so shocked when you all rode up, I'm surprised you remembered what it was."

"Me too, actually. Marcus, I want to thank you."

"Thank me? For what?"

"These past months have been the most difficult of my life. Up until the wedding, I believed that the parts of me that were the most *me* died with Ross. Being with you, being able to feel normal and whole for one night, resurrected something inside me. It gave me hope that one day all that's broken inside will actually heal."

I hesitated as I looked at the basket and then up at the glint in his eyes. He would take me again if I wished it. All the attraction we'd felt for one another that night was still present. It radiated off the walls of the small space we sat in with an intensity that had me ready to give into it, but I wasn't ready. I wasn't sure I ever would be.

"Silva." He leaned forward in his seat and with only the slightest hesitation, reached for my hands. "I'm not here to seduce you. I didn't come here in the hope that we would pick right back up where we left off. I came here to put whatever worry you had over my being here at ease. You are just as free to start over here as you were before you knew you would run into me. I know the kind of baggage that we leave behind when we move on to someplace new. The last thing I would want is for you to feel like you've baggage here, as well."

I didn't know what to say to him. Marcus—I still didn't know his last name—was the sort of man I could fall for. The only sort of man I'd ever seen that could rival Ross. His words were kind and well meant, and while I knew that I wasn't ready for anyone else to come into my life, they also felt like a rejection, and that same spot in my chest that always carried grief began to hurt just a little bit more.

"I see."

He watched me carefully for a moment before withdrawing his hands and leaning back in his seat.

"Our night together was one of the best of my life. Don't take what I said and try to make it mean anything else. I only meant this: You deserve the opportunity to create the life you want here. There was something between us that night, I won't deny it, but I expect nothing from you. I want to be your friend. If in time, something else occurs, then great, but if not, I still want to be your friend, Silva. I want to be the person that you can lean on here, that helps you sort through the muck and the drama that is bound to happen on this isle. And you can't do anything to cause me to retract my friendship. Do you understand? You're free to do whatever you wish, I'm here for you—we are all here for you—no matter what."

Tears I didn't even know I needed to cry came freely then. Before I knew it, he was pulling me up from the chair and into the best hug I'd ever had. He had the most calming presence about him. I'd never seen anyone that could ooze such sex and serenity at once.

"How did you know what I was thinking? It was like you could see me worrying that perhaps you didn't enjoy our night together as much as I did. Is that one of your druid skills? Can you read minds?"

He shrugged and gently gathered my hair together to keep it from getting pulled between my shoulders and his chest. "Not at all, but my best friends have always been female. I guess I've learned to read between the lines a bit in regards to what you all say and what you think. If you watch enough, it's all spelled out on your face."

"You should start classes for other men. Women would pay you to teach their men to be that perceptive. You'd make a killing."

He laughed and gently pulled away.

"I should've thought about that back in Boston. I'm not sure I'd have much success with it here."

He took one step toward the door and I hurried to open it for him.

"Thank you for the food and for everything else. I feel much better."

"Good. That was the goal. I'll be gone in the morning. I have somewhere I have to go with Brachan for a few days, but Laurel and Kate will see you settled in here. When I'm back, let's catch up. You can let me know how it's going."

"I look forward to it."

I stood in the doorway until I could no longer see him. For the first time since Ross' death, I slept through the night without waking.

CHAPTER 12

*S*leep had been a pointless effort. He lay awake thinking of all he'd said to Silva and damning himself for being so idiotic in his selflessness. Of course he would be Silva's friend if that was the only option. And, while she healed, that was all he needed to be. But he didn't *want* to be just her friend forever. She'd been on his mind for every waking moment since their night together. And the revelation about who she truly was only made him want her more. It gave them shared experiences, reference points of their old lives back in the twenty-first century that he would never have with anyone from this time.

"Ye seem distracted, Marcus, and I think it has little to do with the purpose of our journey. Although, speaking of which, ye have yet to tell me where we are going or what 'tis about."

He stirred from his trance as he and Brachan rode together toward the small boat that would take them to the mainland. "I think I'm a fool, Brachan. I'm a stupid, self-sacrificing fool."

Brachan laughed and rode a little closer to him. "Ye are often too selfless for yer own good. I love Kate and Laurel both verra much, but ye do things for them that ye needna do."

It was true, he knew it, but Laurel and Kate were so special to him. There was nothing he wouldn't do for either one of them.

"This time, it actually has nothing to with them."

"Truly? Then what ye've gotten yerself into?"

He'd given Silva his word that he would keep their secret, but if he didn't speak to someone about it he would burst, and Brachan was by far the best candidate.

"I think I've fallen for Murray Castle's newest resident, and I did a fantastic job convincing her that I only wanted to be her friend."

"Already, lad? She only arrived yesterday."

"She only arrived yesterday, but as I told you last night, I met her at the wedding. We got on well, although I never thought I'd see her again. Now that she's here, I can't see how I'll manage to stay away from her."

"The lass needs to heal, Marcus. She's been through much. Once Raudrich tells her the truth, she'll have even more to deal with."

He nodded. As they reached the stables that would house their horses until they returned, they dismounted together.

"I know. But she won't be sad forever, will she? And when she's not, I don't want to already be so hard in the friend zone that there's no coming out of it."

Brachan stared at him with unbridled confusion. "Friend zone? It must be one of yer twenty-first century expressions for I know I've never heard it before."

"Yes, but surely you understand my meaning."

"I do. I'll not pretend to know much of anything when it comes to matters of the heart, but surely ye can be her friend, and give her the space to heal while still giving her clues about how ye may feel. I do know this—if she is meant to love ye, yer patience with her will serve ye well. Show her patience, give her time, and when her heart is ready, she will love ye all the more for yer kindness. Now." Brachan paused and walked toward the stables with his horse. "Tell me where we are going and why. My curiosity is killing me."

He could only hope Brachan was right, that perhaps his patience would one day see him rewarded. For now though, it was time to tell Brachan the truth of his plans to see Freya freed.

---

*N*ot long past dawn, I woke to the sound of knocking on my door, followed by the quick chatter of what sounded like a group of women.

When I opened the door, Laurel stood there with a basket in her hand identical to the now-empty one on the cottage table.

"Sorry if we're disturbing you. We thought perhaps it might be easier for us to give you a gradual introduction to everyone than to throw you into the group headfirst."

I yawned and opened the door to let the group inside. I recognized them all from the wedding, although Laurel was the only one I'd ever spoken to. The younger blonde had to be her sister. If the similarity in their chins and noses were any indication, I assumed the other woman with them was their mother.

"Not at all. Come on in."

Smiling, they filed in.

"Was the food okay last night? I'm sure it wasn't very warm, but hopefully it at least kept you from going to bed hungry."

"It was perfect." I grabbed the basket as Laurel extended it to me.

"We brought you some breakfast. Olivia wandered into the castle this morning and has now been taken captive by Davina, our new groundskeeper's daughter. She was so glad to see someone her age that she didn't really give your stepsister any choice in the matter."

"I'm sure Olivia is also glad to meet someone her age."

"I'm Kate." Laurel's sister extended her left hand and I quickly adjusted to offer her my left hand, as well.

"Silva. It's so nice to meet you. I saw you at the wedding, of course, but we didn't get a chance to meet. I was so busy spontaneously bursting into tears of joy for Laurel, I'm afraid that there were lots of people I didn't speak to. What do you think of the cabin? I designed the interior myself."

"It's wonderful. It's almost like being back home—in the twenty-first century, I mean."

"Then I met my goal. We desperately needed a few spaces around here that didn't scream Stone Age."

"You're only a few millennia off, sis."

Kate rolled her eyes at her sister and huffed. "I never said I was a history buff. You know what I mean."

I stepped toward the third woman as she ignored her daughters and moved toward me.

"And I'm Myla, their mother."

"I'm so pleased to meet all of you." I peeked into the basket to see it stuffed with food. "I hope you all are planning to join me. I definitely can't eat this all myself."

Laurel reached for the basket she'd just handed me and began to lay everything out on the table. "You bet we are. We hoped to give you the rundown of things before you meet everyone at dinner tonight."

Kate spoke as she took a seat at the table. "She won't meet everyone. Brachan and Marcus won't be there. They left this morning."

"Oh really?" Laurel sounded surprised.

"Yes, although I'm not sure where they went. Maddock said that Brachan didn't know and that Marcus was very secretive about all of it."

"Hmm..."

I watched as both women turned to look at their mother suspiciously.

"What? You know something, don't you?"

Myla shrugged and shook her head. "No, I don't know anything for certain. It's only that Marcus has been secretive about everything lately. I wonder if he's convinced Brachan to accompany him while he goes to visit the woman I saw him speaking with at your wedding."

"Woman? What woman?" Both Laurel and Kate said the words in unison as my muscles turned to liquid, and I reached to grip the chair.

"I don't know what woman. I never got a good look at her face, but I saw him visiting with someone at the party. He was clearly quite taken with her. I wouldn't be surprised at all if they continued correspondence after the wedding."

Hoping that my face hadn't blushed with embarrassment, I lowered myself into a seat as I settled in to listen as they made all sorts of guesses about the woman they had no idea was me.

CHAPTER 13

*I*t was the next morning before I had any real chance to check in with Olivia. Laurel, Kate, and Myla had stayed with me until well past midday, and by the time Raudrich finished giving me a tour of the castle and grounds, it was time for dinner. Then after that three-hour-long ordeal, it was time for bed.

Raudrich's behavior while showing me around my new home was strange and unsettling. The normally self-assured man fidgeted endlessly. I eventually stopped counting the number of times he opened his mouth to speak and then stopped. Something was eating at him, and I hadn't the slightest clue what.

Eager to be around the comforting and familiar presence of my stepsister, I went over to her cabin early in the morning to see if she wanted to join me for a walk.

"O'course. I feel as if I havena seen ye at all since we arrived. In truth, while I was pleased at the thought of having my own space, 'tis unsettling to be so alone after never having been so in my whole life."

I smiled and offered her my arm, and we strolled away from the set of cabins behind the castle.

"I was like that the first time I lived on my own, too. You'll get used to it, I promise. And you're always welcome to come and stay with me anytime you wish. So, how are you liking the castle. What was your impression of everyone last night?"

Olivia grinned and I had the sudden sinking sensation that if I didn't watch her closely, she was bound to get into all sorts of trouble here.

"Do ye think they've all taken some sort of beauty potion? I've never seen such a group of handsome men in my life, Silva. Doona ye remember what the men at home look like? Certainly not like that lot."

I laughed and nodded in agreement. While I didn't remember the men in Allen territory being as loathsome looking as Olivia suggested, I was certain that the swoon-worthy gents at her home didn't usually gather around the same table every evening. The dining hall at Murray Castle oozed testosterone. I wasn't even fueled by the same roaring, early-twenties sex hormones as Olivia, and I had to admit that it felt rather overwhelming sitting there amongst them—and that was with two of them missing.

I didn't have to answer Olivia's rhetorical question for her to continue.

"And they all seem so nice."

They did seem that. I'd never been so fussed over as I had been sitting down to eat amongst the legendary members of The Eight.

Nicol, the castle's master, had welcomed us warmly.

Quinn, a man with hair so blond it shouldn't have been naturally occurring outside of a bottle, had ushered us both to our seats while he regaled us with embarrassing stories about the other men.

Ludo had served the meal he'd cooked himself, and you could see the pride that he took in his work. I loved watching him watch everyone else eat. He was delighted each time someone smiled or savored his food.

Raudrich and Maddock we'd both met before, but it was a joy to see them interact with their wives. Although, the bond between them made the empty hole in my own chest ache with a yearning I had to continually shake off all evening so it wouldn't swallow me whole.

Henry, a strong, strapping beast of a man with curly red hair and a beard that I wanted to cut so badly it made my hands twitch, sat in between us. He had an infectious smile. His personality was so at odds with his intimidating appearance that it made him even more likable. I wanted to record his laugh to have on playback for a gloomy day.

"I do think they're all very nice. What did you think of the girl you spent yesterday morning with?"

As if manifested by my words, two figures appeared in the distance. Olivia tried desperately to pull me back the other direction, but we'd already been seen.

"That's her with her father. Let's go back, Silva. I doona wish to be taken hostage again. The lass talked endlessly."

The man next to the girl was waving, and I knew there was nothing we could do to avoid the interaction. I looked over at her and shrugged. "Sorry. We've been spotted. Was she so bad?"

"No, she's a nice girl, but I dinna get a word in all morning."

"'Ello there!" The girl's father bellowed as we neared each other on the path around the castle. I couldn't help but think the man looked like he belonged on a pirate ship. With a deep scar that sliced down the side of his face, several missing teeth, and long, wild hair that draped over his shoulders, all he needed was an eyepatch and a parrot to complete the look.

His hand was already extended toward me as we reached him. When I took it, the tightness of his grip took my breath away.

"Ye must be Silva."

I gasped and swallowed to keep from laughing as he released my hand and moved to shake Olivia's.

"And ye must be Olivia. My sweet Davina hasna stopped speaking about ye since she met ye yesterday. She's right pleased to have a friend here. The move hasna been easy on her. Why, she thinks ye are the kindest, prettiest lass she's ever seen."

I glanced over at Davina to see a bright blush spread over her face as she gently whacked her father's arm.

"Da! Is there nothing I can say to ye that ye willna tell another?"

Pinkie's face dropped momentarily in what I could only assume was regret, but he recovered quickly. "I'm sorry, lass. 'Tis only that I'm pleased that someone has arrived that might be yer friend."

I glanced over at the dreadful expression on Olivia's face and hurried to try and save her in any way I could. "Your name is Pinkie, correct? Laurel told me how knowledgeable you are about all of the trees and plants around here. Liv has a keen interest in such stuff."

Pinkie's eyes lit up. "Aye. I know ye wouldna think it, with me being a former tavern owner and all, but the land is my first love. 'Tis it true, Olivia? If so, I can tell ye all about the trees surrounding yer wee cottage right now."

I winked at Olivia. Catching my meaning, she stepped toward Pinkie.

"Aye, I would love to hear about them."

As Pinkie and Liv walked a few steps in front of us, I fell behind with Davina to try to occupy her so that she might give Olivia a break. In truth, I felt rather sorry for her. Pinkie's personality was so boisterous, I suspected the only time Davina ever got a real word in was when her father wasn't around. No wonder she'd talked Olivia's ear off the day before.

"Has it always just been you and your father?"

Davina nodded as she kept pace with me. "Aye. My ma died when I was just a bairn."

"I was raised by my father too. I never knew my mom."

"Truly?"

"Yes. It's tough sometimes, isn't it? My dad's a lot like that, too. His personality fills a room."

Seeing that we had something in common seemed to warm

Davina to me, and it didn't take long before she spoke freely. The girl had many interests, most of which I never would have expected. Many in this time—despite the prevalence of it—were quite skittish around anything involving witchcraft or the unexplainable. Not Davina. She told stories of mystics and witches and talked about her desire to study the stars. She was well read, which gave me a new respect for her father that I didn't quite have at first impression. He'd taught his daughter to read and encouraged her to explore whatever interested her. Despite his weathered appearance, Pinkie was a man ahead of his time.

"So, books, horseback riding, what else interests you?"

She glanced down at her feet as another blush creeped over her skin.

"Oh, I know that look. Is there a boy, then?"

"Not a boy, miss. A man. The finest man I've ever seen."

I smiled. "Are you and this man sweethearts?"

She shook her head sadly. "No."

"Does he know that you care for him?"

"No, not at all."

"Hm." I stopped and crossed my arms as I turned to look at her. "Let me give you a little piece of advice. Men aren't very good at picking up subtle clues. Don't overdo it, of course, but make sure to speak to him when you're around him. If there's ever a reason for you to touch his arm or brush your shoulder against his, take it. Sometimes they just need a little help seeing what's right in front of them."

"Ye are right. I never speak to him."

"Well, there you go then. You have some place to start now."

About fifty yards ahead, Pinkie called out over his shoulder to his daughter. "Come, Davina. We must be back in the village soon."

He waved a goodbye as Davina walked away, and Olivia returned to my side.

"What did ye say to make her smile like that?"

"I only gave her some advice about a boy she seems rather smitten with."

Olivia stepped in front of me and shook her head. "Did she tell ye who 'tis she fancies?"

"No."

"'Tis Marcus, Silva. Ye just pushed her towards yer wedding-time lover."

CHAPTER 14

One Week Later

*M*arcus arrived in the dining hall early hoping to meet Silva when she entered. He knew just visiting with her would cheer him up.

Their trip had been a pointless one. The man he'd read about in one of the castle's many books was dead—and had been for over twenty years. He'd known it was possible—probable even—but he still believed it worth checking in to. Had the man lived, he would've been a good source of information. An expert in faerie lore, Marcus had hoped that he might be able to give him some idea of how to free Freya from Machara's grasp.

She entered the room just after Nicol, and he hurried to her side before anyone else showed up to pull her away.

"You're back!"

It pleased him that she was glad to see he'd returned, and he smiled as he walked her over to the table.

"Yes. I'm afraid it was a wasted trip."

"I'm sorry."

He dismissed it. He didn't want to speak about him. Each day while away, he'd wondered how she was doing, if she was enjoying her time at the castle, if she would decide to stay.

"It's fine. I'll find what I need to in the end. How are you and Olivia finding everything here? Are you ready to leave yet?" He pulled out a chair for her before sitting down at her side.

"No, not at all. Both Olivia and I have settled in quite well."

Her smile was bright but her tone seemed off. He searched her expression for the words she didn't say. It was one he recognized from his early days at the castle.

"The people are nice, the grounds beautiful, but you're bored out of your mind?"

She turned and tipped her head to the side as she frowned suspiciously at him. "Are you sure you don't read minds?"

She had no idea how much he wished he truly could read hers.

"Quite sure. I just remember what it was like here at the castle before my powers started showing up. Back when we thought Morna sent us here just for Laurel, I had no real purpose, nothing to pass the days with. It's not an easy thing when you're accustomed to being busy. You were running Allen territory on your own. I'm sure that you never had a moment to yourself. Even if you are in need of some rest, it has to be strange to change your pace so quickly."

She looked at him for the briefest moment without saying anything. In the small space of silence, he swore he could feel her soul reaching out to his.

"I keep hearing so much about this Morna woman. I hope one day to meet her, and yes, the sudden change in activity is hard for me to deal with."

He could scarcely believe that Silva hadn't met Morna either.

"I have absolutely no doubt that you'll meet her one day. She can't seem to stay out of anyone's business for very long."

She looked away from him as the table around them filled.

Knowing they would have little chance to visit once the meal began, he leaned in to make her an offer he hoped she wouldn't refuse.

"I could use some help if you'd like something to keep you busy."

She reached out and squeezed his hand underneath the table. "Absolutely. What is it?"

"Meet me outside the stables after dinner, and I'll tell you all about it. You can decide then if you're interested."

She retracted her hand and smiled at him. "I'll be interested."

He hoped so. It would give him more time with her, which he wanted more than anything, and he truly could use the help.

Marcus' arrival back at the castle and his offer was a godsend. Three times over the last week, I'd gone to Raudrich and begged him to give me something to do, but each time he insisted that he still felt guilty for putting so much work on me in Allen territory and that all he wanted for me now was to rest and enjoy. He seemed to be deaf to the fact that resting never brought me much joy.

Dinner lasted no longer than usual, but it seemed to drag on forever. I was anxious to talk to Marcus. I was pleased that by the time I reached the stables, he was already there waiting for me.

"Okay, what is it? I'm ready to start helping now, if you wish."

He waved me over. As I approached, he grabbed my shoulders to position me in front of him so that my back was against his chest. With his arms reaching around me, he pointed through the glassed-in garden to a spot near its center. I hoped he couldn't feel or hear the acceleration of my breath as his arms brushed my shoulders.

"Have you met Freya yet?"

I knew the story of Murray Castle's ghostly resident. Raudrich had told Ross and me everything long ago.

"No. Laurel mentioned that Nicol stays with her at night, so I didn't wish to intrude on their time together."

"He should be, but lately he's been more and more absent. I come to visit with her on the nights he is away."

He didn't step away as we watched her, and secretly, I was glad. The evening air was cool and his arms were warm around me.

"Is that what you want me to do? Visit with her when Nicol is away?" He reached for my shoulders once more and spun me toward him before stepping away towards the garden. "No. How much do you know about Machara and our purpose here?"

While I knew the story surrounding both of them, Machara and Freya were the only two residents of the castle I'd yet to meet. It had never felt right to interrupt Nicol and Freya's time together—not when I believed they actually were spending time together. And both Laurel and Raudrich had insisted that Machara was now weaker than she'd been in years. The fact that they'd all vowed to stay away from her and leave her in total isolation only added to her weakened state. Since I had no desire to do anything to help the bitch, I'd been able to curb my overly curious nature and stay away from her.

"I know everything. Raudrich told me much of it before, and over the past week, Laurel, Kate, and Myla have filled in the things he left out."

He nodded as if he expected as much. "Freya is fading right along with Machara. I can't just let her die without trying to help her. As I'm sure you've learned in the past week, we rotate duties in the castle. We do our best to spread our work evenly, but it seems that I have a penchant for working the garden that the other men do not. It has been my full assignment for some time. I was wondering if you'd like to split my daily garden work with me. For the first few weeks I can teach you. Once you're comfortable, I can use the time you're tending the garden to continue my research in the library and search for some clue as to what we can do to save Freya from her fate."

"Does anyone else know?"

"Only Brachan." He smiled and then teased. "We all know you're good at keeping a secret. I knew it would be safe to tell you. I don't want any of the others to know until I know whether or not it's even possible. I don't want to get Nicol's hopes up, and I don't want anyone else to try and talk me out of at least trying."

"I'll help. I'll be glad to." I could think of nothing more useful that I could do at the castle. I didn't know anything about plants, but I could learn anything with the right teacher.

"Great. Then, let's go meet Freya. You'll love her. Everyone does."

*F*reya opened her mouth to speak, but Marcus quickly held up a hand to stop her. "Wait until she's gone, Freya."

He watched as Silva made her way out of the garden. Once the door closed behind her, he faced Freya.

"She's lovely."

"She is."

"And ye are certain ye only mean to teach her to garden to relieve her boredom? It has nothing to do with yer desire to be near her?"

He shrugged unapologetically. "Perhaps it's both."

She smiled. "I hope she deserves ye. God knows 'tis yer turn."

He only hoped he was deserving of her, and that with time, she would see it.

CHAPTER 15

December

hey say time heals all wounds, but I never quite believed that until I came to The Isle of Eight Lairds and Murray Castle. While I now knew that I would never stop missing Ross, I could sense that my need for him lessened with each passing day. Something about The Isle and its strange, but kind, group of men, something about the time to myself, something about the minimal responsibility of tending to Freya's gorgeous garden for a few hours each day, was slowly working to bring me back to life.

It was November when I first noticed it—the sudden realization as I lay down to sleep that Ross hadn't crossed my mind until that point in the day. Or at least, if he had, the memory hadn't been so painful that it knocked me to my knees.

It didn't take long for Olivia and me to settle into our individual routines on The Isle, and before long, days became weeks that became months.

Each morning, I would rise at dawn and Olivia and I would

walk the path on the outer edge of the castle grounds where we would gossip and catch up—fill each other in on our plans for the day. After parting, I would start my shift in Freya's garden, working diligently until midday when Marcus would collect me. Then the two of us would walk a similar path.

While my conversations with Liv were easy, I wasn't sure Marcus knew how to be with anyone in such an easy and superficial way. It seemed to me that if Marcus wished to talk, he wished to talk meaningfully. It was easy to see why Laurel adored him so completely. He truly cared. He wanted to know, wanted to understand, wanted to help in whatever way he could.

I was constantly surprised by the way his mind worked, by the thought he put into everything he did and said, by the questions he asked me. By the time the first snow fell on Murray Castle, I had begun to wonder if anyone else in my life had ever sought to know me in the same way Marcus did.

A fortnight before Christmas, I knew the truth.

I was in love with him.

The trouble was, every time I let that one dangerous thought slip in, I began to hate myself.

It was too soon for me to feel this way about anyone. Ten months surely wasn't enough time for me to grieve, not when Ross had been my entire world for so long. Each flutter of my heart when Marcus brushed against me, each time I longed to reach out and grab his hand, I felt as if I were betraying Ross' memory.

"So? What do you think?"

I wasn't sure how long I'd been zoned out, but I knew it was long enough for me to not have a clue what he was asking me. It took him only a moment to read my guilty expression.

"Where are you, Silva?"

"I'm so sorry. What did you ask?"

"It was nothing. Hey, you look as if you need to get out of here for a bit. Want to help me with something after dinner tonight? I'm afraid it's not going to be a fun task."

Anything was more fun than being stuck in my own head.

"Absolutely. What are we doing?"

"Spying on Nicol. Freya is convinced that he's taken a lover. That on nights when he's not with her, he's in the village with someone else. I don't want to believe it, but he has become more withdrawn lately, more angry, and he visits Freya less and less."

"What will you do if Freya's right?"

"Nothing, but I'd like to know all the same."

"I'm in."

*N*icol wasn't with another woman. We followed him to a part of The Isle I'd yet to see and stayed back when he dismounted and walked to a snow-covered hill where he dropped to his knees and called out to someone unseen.

"Take me. Return Paton to us and ye can have me forever. I'll not ever stop coming here. Canna ye see it? I will shout through this veil until ye hear me and come."

"What is he doing?" I whispered the question in Marcus' ear and then turned my ear toward his mouth so he could answer me.

"He's calling for Machara's father. The veil is thinnest here. It's where Paton sacrificed himself for Kate. He's trying to get him back."

"Will it work?"

Marcus seemed so certain that it broke my heart a little to see Nicol screaming at the top of his lungs for nothing.

"No. Paton promised Machara's father three years. We will not see him one day before then."

After calling out to Paton's captor, Nicol knelt in silence.

"Then why does he do it?"

"Helplessness is not an emotion anyone handles well. Nicol can't help Freya, and he knows it. Perhaps he believes that if he can help Paton, the sacrifice of himself would be worth it."

We watched him until nearly dawn. Nicol never moved, and Machara's father never answered him.

When we finally turned to leave him, Marcus solemnly whispered, "We can never tell anyone about this. This is his secret. His alone."

I never wanted to speak of it again. Nicol's entire life was one of suffering and guilt. The last thing he needed to feel was embarrassment for trying to help in whatever way he could.

"I know."

CHAPTER 16

"*I* got you something."

I hadn't heard him enter the garden, or even approach, but I didn't jump at the sound of his voice. I merely smiled and brushed the soil from my hands before pushing myself up from my knees so I could face him.

"The fountain over there really drowns everything else out. I like it."

He laughed and I noticed that his hands were behind his back. "It's pretty enough, but I can't listen to the running water for more than half an hour without needing to pee."

I pointed behind his back. "Whatcha hiding?"

"Your Christmas present."

"You do know that Christmas is still ten days away, right?"

He nodded but didn't move his arms. "I do, but Brachan and I are getting ready to leave again. A while back I wrote to one of Brachan's contacts back in the town where he grew up. Brachan thought perhaps his friend might know the name of someone who could help us. He's replied. He knows of a couple who lives on the western coast of the mainland that might be able to help us. I'm afraid the trip will keep us away over Christmas, but we should be back by the new year."

I couldn't hide my disappointment that they would be away, even if it was for a good reason. "Are you sure you can't wait until New Years' to leave? Laurel and Kate have all sorts of celebrations planned over the next few weeks."

"I know exactly what they've got planned. While I will be sad to miss it, I've spent many Christmases with them, and I'm afraid the couple we seek never stays in one place for too long. I don't want to risk missing them while we know where they are."

Eager for something to lift my suddenly blue spirits, I attempted to reach behind his back, but he quickly moved out of the way.

"Hey, now. No, you don't. No peeking."

I dropped my hands and stood still. "Well, are you going to show me or not?"

He nodded and slowly moved his hands to the front. A beautiful red afghan draped across his left forearm.

"You mentioned a while back that one of the things you missed most from home was our softer fabrics. I remember thinking what a remarkable thing it was for you to say. You could've said television or hot running water, but all you really wanted was something truly soft to wrap yourself up in."

He shook his head and I couldn't tell if he thought me ridiculous or admired my response.

"Anyway, there's a woman down in the village that makes all sorts of bedding and linens. I had her send for some softer fabric weeks ago. I won't pretend I made this myself, but I did have it made just for you."

I reached for it and buried my face in the fabric as I brought it close.

It was the most wonderful thing I'd held in ages.

"It's perfect. Absolutely perfect."

He opened his arms to me as I hugged him.

"I'll run this over to your cabin before Brachan and I leave."

"Are you leaving right away?"

"Yes, we are. See you around New Year's?"

"Marcus." I continued to hold on to him as I spoke. "Promise me that you guys will stop somewhere at night. Find an inn each night so you can escape from the frigid weather. It's dangerously cold out there."

He rubbed my back gently. "I promise you we'll try. I have no desire to stay outdoors during winter, either, but I'm afraid it's not as easy as us just deciding to stay somewhere."

"Why is that?"

He pulled away and pointed to himself.

"There were still many places in the twenty-first century I didn't always feel welcome, but here..." He hesitated and shook his head. "Well, we are still many, many years before things even start to get a little better for black people."

I felt foolish that it hadn't occurred to me before. The Isle was such a secluded place. With Nicol and The Eight serving as complete authority on The Isle, they were able to create the world they wanted here. It was easy to forget the rest of the world didn't work the same way.

"Is it...is it safe for you to leave here?"

"Definitely."

His tone was confident and that helped to ease the knot in my chest slightly.

"I'll be fine. I can promise you that. I have magic. So does Brachan. No one is going to harm either of us. It's just not always pleasant. There's a good chance we will be turned away from wherever we try to stay."

Just knowing it was a possibility infuriated me. "I hate it."

He nodded. All I wanted to do was throw my arms around him once more and beg him to just stay here. Or at least let me come with him so I could kick anyone's ass that gave him a hard time.

"I know. Me too. I'm just thankful that most days it's not an issue here. And at least I can stop anyone from being a real threat thanks to my magic. Most don't have that option."

"You guys just hurry back, okay? We will all be eagerly awaiting you New Year's."

I stared at him a long moment. As he turned to leave, I quickly pulled him back around toward me so that I could kiss his cheek goodbye. I'd be counting the minutes until he returned.

---

*M*arcus stood back as he watched the usually unflappable Brachan lose his cool on the cold-faced, blatantly racist innkeeper.

"What do ye mean, ye have no rooms? There isna a single patron in yer tavern. If ye had even one room occupied, ye would have people down below, but ye doona, do ye? 'Twould be a mistake to turn us away."

"I'm sorry. I doona mean either of ye harm, but I've no rooms for the likes of ye."

Marcus reached forward and grabbed at Brachan's arm as he watched his friend's fist tighten into a ball. "Let's just keep going. We can spare a little magic to give our horses strength and keep us warm for the night."

As Brachan turned to face him, the innkeeper closed the door in their faces.

"I know we've the magic, but 'tis the principle of it."

"While I appreciate where you're coming from, we're not going to change history or the way people think by breaking that old idiot's nose."

"Psst..."

The sound came from behind him. As Brachan leaned to the side to look toward the noise, Marcus faced it.

A boy not much older than twenty stood a few yards away, a lantern in his hand to light up the night.

"Old man Aklen is a horse's arse. If ye need a place to stay, ye can follow me. I've stables and a warm home."

"Ye do?"

Brachan seemed skeptical, and Marcus didn't miss the way the boy hesitated slightly before answering.

"Aye. 'Twas my da's but he's long since passed. 'Tis mine now. Come on. I've even a recent kill we can roast on the fire."

Marcus stepped toward the boy and offered him his hand. "Are you sure? It would be much appreciated."

The boy took his hand and Marcus smiled at his strong grip.

"Aye, quite sure. I'm Jimmie."

"I'm Marcus. This is Brachan. We are just passing through the village. We will be on our way in the morning."

Jimmie stepped away and began to lead them to the last home at the edge of the village. The lad's father must have been a successful trader for it was the nicest home by far.

Brachan clasped the lad on the shoulder once they reached the stable. "Thank ye, lad. It means more than ye can possibly know."

"'Tis Christmas. 'Tis the least I can do for ye. Aklen would do good to remember it."

CHAPTER 17

"Are you ever going to tell me what's the matter? You never come to the garden, yet you've been watching me work in here all morning. I can see it on your face, Liv. You know as well as I do that you'll feel better if you just spit it out."

She looked as solemn-faced as I'd ever seen her, although I'd seen this breakdown coming for weeks now. The initial attraction of being away from home had worn off, and I now suspected she felt rather lost.

"I think 'twould be ungrateful of me to express how I feel."

"Don't worry about that with me. There's no right or wrong way to feel. You can't help how you feel about anything."

She stared at me, crossed her arms, and dropped to the floor so that we were eye level with each other.

"Ye did just hear the words that came out of yer mouth, dinna ye? Why doona ye take yer own advice? Then mayhap I'll be more inclined to listen to ye."

I'd said nothing to Olivia about my conflicting emotions, but it seemed that Marcus wasn't the only one who found me remarkably easy to read.

"What do you mean?"

She took the watering pail from me and grabbed my hand to help me up from the ground.

"If ye believed 'twas fine for ye to feel the way ye feel, ye would be back in Marcus' bed by now."

I hoped no one else was able to see how much I cared for him.

"Is it that obvious?"

She shook her head. "Only to me."

"Well, that's some comfort, but I don't want to talk about me, Liv. Haven't you heard the expression, 'do as I say, not as I do?' Now, what's up?"

She sighed and covered her face with her hands. "I'm so pleased to be away from home. I truly am. I canna tell ye how thankful I am that ye allowed me to come with ye. I enjoy the freedom I have here. I love the castle, the people, and staying alone in the cabin is no longer as strange as it once was, but Silva, I am not content.

"I know 'tis foolish, but part of me believed that leaving home would force my life to begin. I doona know what I'm meant to do, where I'm meant to be. I only know that I need more in my days than wandering about the castle and gossiping with Davina. I'm restless, and I canna bear it much longer."

Of course she was restless. Olivia was young. She needed adventure, and as hesitant as I was to admit it, even a little bit of trouble. At least back home, she had her pursuit of rebellion to keep her busy. Here there was nothing for her to rebel against. Without that distraction, she was quickly losing her mind.

"You need to work, Liv. Why don't we speak to Raudrich and see if he can give you something to busy yourself with? Or perhaps, we can go down to the village and see if we can find something respectable for you to do?"

I might as well have suggested that she eat worms. She looked disgusted.

"I doona think work will solve anything."

Brushing the dirt from my hands, I leaned back to look at her. "Why are you so sure of that? Work helps just about anything."

"How old were ye when ye first fell in love, Silva?"

I smiled at her as her brow creased. "Ah. That's the thing then."

"Ye dinna answer my question."

"You won't like my answer. Ross was the first man I truly ever loved. I was twenty-seven."

To Olivia, twenty-seven surely seemed ancient.

"I doona believe ye."

"It's true. Now, I definitely fell in lust a few times before that, but love, not so much."

"I wish to fall in lust, then."

"No, you don't. It's not worth it, I promise you. It's still quite possible to end up with a broken heart even if you aren't in love."

"Well, then let my heart be broken. I just need something, Silva —something to make me feel as if I'm the woman that I am. Will ye take me somewhere?"

"Where?"

"Davina spoke of a traveling fortune teller that will have a tent set up in the woods the day after tomorrow. She only comes to The Isle once every three years, for many here doona accept what she does. Davina and her father are going. Will ye take me?"

I could think of nothing less appealing than hearing my future. After all the pain of the past year, I was more than happy to just take things day by day.

"Why would you want to learn your future? If she speaks good news, all you will do is live in anticipation. If it's bad, it will fill you with fear. Either way, it takes the joy out of the day you're living right now."

She didn't appear convinced.

"'Twill do neither of those things. I only wish to know how long I must wait. If 'tis another decade, then I shall make my peace with it. If 'tis soon then I shall ready my heart for it."

Skeptical, I sat in silence just long enough to drive Liv crazy. The likelihood of the woman's predictions being any more than faerie tales was slim. Surely, giving Olivia one night of entertainment wouldn't hurt.

"Okay, fine, but you must promise me that you won't put too much weight in anything she tells you, okay? Ask Davina if we can accompany her and her father. I don't want us to wander off into the woods on our own since we aren't very familiar with The Isle."

She smiled and pushed herself up from the ground. "I promise. Thank ye, Silva. Thank ye, thank ye, thank ye."

She bent to kiss the top of my head and quickly skipped out of the garden.

---

*T*here was an eerie feeling to the woman's tent. I couldn't deny it no matter how much I wanted to. Only a small crowd—the most eccentric residents of The Isle—waited outside for their turn with the mysterious woman. The closer it came to our turn inside the tent, the more I wanted to retreat back to the castle. My dread doubled with each passing minute.

"Liv, I'll go inside if you want me to, but I don't want a reading, okay?"

She watched me carefully and reached out to squeeze my arm. "Doona tell me ye are frightened? Ye told me just this morning that ye dinna believe in this."

I didn't want to believe in it, but the truth was, after everything that had happened in my life, I found it hard to disbelieve anything outright.

"Not frightened—just anxious. I'll accompany you, but I've no desire to be read by her."

The quick rustle of fabric preceded Pinkie and Davina's exit from the tent. Neither looked too traumatized and my nerves relaxed just enough to help me take the next step toward the tent Liv seemed so determined to enter.

The soothsayer's setup was simple and bare. Rather than the

pile of pillows and scattered candles I was expecting, the tent was lit with just enough light so that we could see the outline of the woman as we approached her. She sat at a small wooden table with a candle lit at its corner. Two chairs sat opposite her.

"Ye should leave. I've no room for such energy here."

I twisted to look behind me to see if anyone had entered the tent behind us. It was only when I turned back to see Liv staring at me that I realized the old woman meant me.

"I...I don't know what you mean."

The woman stood and extended a dimly lit finger in my direction. "Ye doona wish to be here, lass. Yer dread has filled this room and I've no need of it. I shall read the young one, but not ye. Go and leave us be."

Shrugging, I turned to do as the old woman instructed. She read me correctly. I would rather be just about anywhere else.

Before I could step away, Olivia reached for my arm.

"Please don't make her leave. She does wish to be here. I promise she does."

I shook my head and tried to wave Olivia on without me, but my stepsister only tightened her grip and pulled me deeper into the tent as the soothsayer spoke once more.

"No, lass. She doesna. She is frightened of me and rightly so. With such an energy hanging over the lass, the reading is bound to bring her unwanted news. Something within her senses it. If she is not ready for it, she should go."

Olivia leaned in to speak to me in a half-whisper. "Did ye hear that, Silva? Ye canna tell me that ye are not a little curious as to what she might tell ye?"

"Not in the slightest."

The old woman laughed and beckoned us forward with a wave of her hand. "If ye will try and release some of yer fear, I will allow ye to stay as I read the fortune of the younger lass. I shall say nothing of yer own future if ye doona wish to hear it."

Immediately, my fear subsided, and I nodded as I let out a shaky breath and followed Olivia over to the two wooden chairs in front of the woman.

Once we were seated, she directed every bit of her attention to Olivia, allowing me to watch on in curious fascination.

"Will ye allow me to take yer hand, lass?"

Olivia didn't hesitate as she put both hands on the table. "Do ye mean my palms?"

"No. I doona read palms. All I need is for my skin to touch yers, and I shall be able to sense the question ye most wish for me to answer. If we are fortunate, I shall see what I need to in order to answer yer question, as well."

Olivia jumped a little as the old woman enveloped Liv's slender fingers within her own, and for the longest moment, we all sat in silence.

After some time, the woman opened her eyes, nodded gently, and smiled before she spoke. "Yer life will change much more quickly than ye realize, lass. Be hopeful for the coming year, for it shall arrive with yer dreams in tow."

Olivia beamed before squealing in response to the fortuneteller's words. "Are ye certain?"

"Aye, though I shall give ye this warning, lass. Answered dreams rarely complete us in the way we hope they shall. Ye would do well to learn more about yerself before ye give yerself to someone else."

I knew firsthand just how right the mystic was about that. Ross' love had just about devoured me whole, and I'd spent so much more time alone—time learning about who I was and what I wanted—before meeting him than Olivia could even fathom now. If I'd met him when I'd been Olivia's age, I'm not sure I would've survived his loss. There wouldn't have been enough of *me* in the relationship to begin with to remain standing after he was gone.

I understood her desire to be loved, to feel alive and wanted, and to be free, but love was a dangerous thing. If I was honest, I didn't much care for the mystic's reading. For Olivia's sake, I hoped it was quite a long time before such love found its way to her.

I could tell that Olivia didn't know how to respond to the woman's warning, and I suspected she didn't wish to ask any more questions for fear that any further revelations from the mystic might deflate the hope that had suddenly swelled up within her.

"I will try to learn something new every day, miss. Thank ye for the reading."

The woman nodded and stood once more. "Ye may leave payment with my man outside."

For the first time since we sat down, the woman glanced over in my direction. The small hairs on my arm stood up.

"Breathe, lass. I'll not read ye, but I'll not be able to sleep if I doona at least tell ye this." She leaned in closer. As if pulled by some invisible magnet, I leaned toward her in return. "What ye believed ye laid to rest on the top of that mountain haunts ye still. Unfinished business hangs over ye like a cloud, lass. With all ye know now, there is naught ye can do to change it. There is so much ye doona know."

Raudrich's revelation that Ross had known about the portal at Cagair had unearthed unfinished business between me and my late husband. I was angry with him for lying to me, for keeping secrets that shouldn't have been only his. I knew that had to be what the woman meant. She'd somehow seen a glimpse of what Raudrich had told me.

The possibility that she meant something else entirely set me on edge, probably because I'd held the same suspicions myself for some time.

Was it possible that Ross had kept even more secrets from me? Secrets that only time would bring to the surface?

CHAPTER 18

"*J* canna tell if ye are pleased or distraught by what we've learned."

Marcus didn't answer Brachan right away. His mind was desperately trying to make sense of everything. The old druid and his wife had spoken in riddles. He couldn't begin to guess how much of what they'd told them was actually true.

"I am overwhelmed by it. If they are correct, then the only way to return Freya to life is to do the one thing that we all believed would truly kill her—Machara must be defeated. How can both things be true?"

Marcus watched as Brachan considered the question. It was one of the things Marcus admired most about Brachan—he never said anything without thought. He wished he were more like that himself.

"I doona believe that both *are* true. Instead, I took their words to mean that where we once thought only one outcome was possible, there are now two. If we do nothing, if we doona learn the spell that can save Freya, she will die when Machara does. If we keep searching and find the magic we are missing, then she can be saved."

Marcus thought on something else the druid had told them—if Freya's body was now decayed to bone, she could never be saved from her current state.

"Assuming Freya's body remains intact where it is buried."

Brachan nodded slowly. "Aye, but I am not so worried about that. If I've any understanding of the way Machara thinks, then Freya's body will be as whole as 'twas the day Machara spelled her. Machara must know that there is a way to return Freya to life. If so, she would never destroy something that gives her the power to bargain with Nicol."

Marcus suspected that Brachan was right, but he dreaded finding out for certain. If Freya's body was now only bone, it would break his heart in a way he wasn't prepared for. But even if her body was whole, they still had so many other problems to solve.

"What about the women, Brachan? We all know that we do not possess the power to defeat Machara. Nine women hold the power. We know some have already come and done their part, but what about the rest? Freya is fading more each day. I'm afraid that if we leave it up to time to bring these women to The Isle, Freya will be gone long before Machara is."

Brachan sighed and pulled his horse to a stop. Marcus quickly did the same.

"Might I speak plainly with ye, Marcus? Ever since Raudrich spoke to us of Silva and her husband, a nagging suspicion has bothered me."

"Always."

"Do ye ever find it strange that ye are here with us?"

Marcus couldn't hold back the snort of laughter that rose up at Brachan's question. "Every damn day."

"I doona believe 'twas ye who was meant to be here."

He was happy in his life, no matter how unexpected it was. It felt right—strange as it was—that he should be here.

"Why do you say that?"

"Why would a man born centuries ahead of this time, a man

who never had any inkling of magic within him before arriving here, be destined to join a legendary group of men bound to this isle? I canna believe all has happened as 'twas meant to."

Marcus frowned as he thought of Laurel and Kate. Their destinies were so clearly tied to The Isle it was unquestionable, and they had been born hundreds of years in the future.

"What about Laurel and Kate? Do you believe they are here because something has gone awry, as well?"

Brachan shook his head, dismounted, and stepped away from his horse to walk and stretch. Marcus joined him.

"No. I believe there were souls that needed them here. Machara wasna the only destiny that awaited them on The Isle."

"That seems a rather romantic notion for you to have—that love is the reason they were tied to this time?"

Brachan shrugged, and Marcus thought he saw his friend's cheeks flush in slight embarrassment.

"I may not have much experience with love, but I know the power of it. Besides, look who 'tis that ye have fallen in love with—a lassie from yer verra own time. Mayhap she isna meant to be here either."

Marcus wasn't following. "What do you mean?"

"Raudrich believes that Ross must have always had magic, while yers dinna show up until ye arrived here. Ross ran from something—mayhap 'twas his duty. Mayhap Ross was meant to be one of The Eight, and ye and Silva were meant to find one another in yer own time. If Ross was meant to be one of us, he would never have met Silva in yer time. She would never have been here."

Brachan's theory was a stretch. Yes, Raudrich had told them that Ross had left Allen territory for a long time, but that didn't necessarily mean he was running from anything.

Before he could voice his doubt, Brachan spoke again.

"I may verra well be wrong, but none of us will know until we find this man and speak to him. Something is off. Otherwise, I canna believe that any man would leave his wife as he did. She needs to know the truth. I canna believe Raudrich has allowed this to go on so long without her knowing. Ye heard Raudrich speak of how powerful Ross' powers must be for him to have been able to hide them so well. Even if he was never meant to be one of The Eight, what if he has the power to save Freya?"

Dread settled in Marcus' gut. He'd intended to speak to Raudrich for weeks now—to demand that he tell Silva the truth about her husband, but he always found it far too easy to talk himself out of such a conversation.

With each passing day, he could see Silva healing. Her smiles came more easily. Her brow was far less furrowed. She was opening herself to him more, as well. While he'd never pushed her, he sensed she was as attracted to him as he was to her. In time, he knew they would find their way to one another just as they had the night of Laurel and Raudrich's wedding.

But once Silva learned of her husband's betrayal, Marcus knew she would slip back into the abyss from which she'd just emerged. He couldn't stand the thought of seeing Silva so broken.

But what if Brachan was right? What if Ross' magic was strong enough to free Freya? Was he so selfish that he would sacrifice Freya's chance at returning to her old life?

He knew that he wasn't. Besides, how would Silva feel if she found out that he had known the truth about her husband all along and hadn't told her?

It was time for everything to come out in the open. The truth had to be told for everyone's sake.

"You're right. The moment we return, I will speak with Raudrich. If he doesn't agree to tell Silva right away, then I'll tell her myself."

*T*he home of the young man who'd given them shelter before glowed like a beacon as they passed through the same small, unfriendly town on their way back home. Marcus couldn't wait to knock on the boy's door and be invited inside to sit by the fire. He'd make sure the boy was paid for his hospitality, but he had no doubt that the boy would open his home to them once again.

Tired and starving, Marcus dismounted as they neared the home and took off at a jog to knock on the door. It only took a moment for the door to fly open.

"Aye? What do ye want?"

Rather than the tall, skinny fair-skinned boy he expected, a bearded, red-faced man with a terrible scowl answered the door.

Shocked, Marcus struggled to answer the stranger that stood before him.

"Forgive me. We were looking for Jimmie. Does he...does he live here?"

The man snorted and shook his head. "Is that what he told ye? The boy is a liar and a thief. I travel away from my home for a fortnight, and the lad breaks into my home and pretends 'tis his home."

Shocked, Marcus looked back uncomfortably over his shoulder at the sound of Brachan's voice.

"Do ye know where we might find the lad?"

The man nodded and pointed to the stables behind the house.

"Aye. Tied up with my horses. And with my horses is where he shall stay. I'll not have either of ye going to see him. He's agreed to work for me for six weeks in exchange for me not turning him over to our laird for a beating, but I doona trust him. At night, I tie him up so he willna leave."

Marcus' teeth clenched together in anger. "You can't just keep someone prisoner."

The man laughed. Marcus jerked away from Brachan's hand that had just landed on his shoulder.

"I'm not keeping him prisoner. I gave the lad a choice. He could work to make amends for entering my home and living off my means, or he could be beaten for his crime. He agreed to stay."

"Then why do you have him tied?"

The man began to close the door as he spoke. "I already told ye, the boy will leave otherwise. Now, leave my home. If ye know Jimmie, ye are no friend of mine."

Seething, Marcus walked away from the home and began to pace around his horse in circles.

He only stopped when he heard Brachan laughing.

"Are ye truly so surprised, Marcus? The lad was not a verra good liar. He dinna know where anything was inside the home, and he never seemed at ease while we were here. In truth, I only hoped that we'd get lucky and the true owner of the home would still be gone by the time we passed back through."

It had never crossed Marcus' mind that the home hadn't belonged to the boy. "Yes, I'm surprised. It never occurred to me that the boy was lying."

Brachan had already mounted his horse and was riding in the direction of the stables.

"Aye, he was, but I suspect the lad had good reason. Regardless, he helped us when no one else would. Let's free him and bring him with us. We can always use good men around the castle."

New Year's Eve

*W*hile our trip to the mystic had done much to improve Olivia's temperament, the woman's words had only served to make me even more uneasy about everything than I already was. The portal at Cagair wasn't Ross' only lie. There were more lies, worse ones, ones that I knew would upend my life once again when they were uncovered.

Did I want to uncover them? I honestly wasn't sure. My life at Castle Murray had been more enjoyable than I'd dreamed possible. Would it really be so wrong for me to truly let go of everything in my past?

"Hurry and get your ale glass ready, Silva. It's nearly midnight."

I stirred as Laurel cheerfully grabbed my shoulder, stirring me from my thoughts.

It seemed almost serendipitous to me that such a choice would lay before me at the start of a new year. I could search and prod and seek out anything and everything that Ross had hidden from me, or I could accept that perhaps I'd only known part of the man I'd married and simply let it all go.

I stood to make my way over to the table where Henry stood pouring ale for everyone when I noticed riders approaching the stables.

Marcus was finally home.

I don't think I even realized just how much I'd missed him. In that moment, I knew exactly what I wanted to do with my new year—I wanted to let the past, every last bit of it, finally go.

"Here ye go, lass. Best join the others so we can toast to the New Year."

I smiled at how well these seventeenth century Scots had adjusted to Laurel and Kate's introduction to more modern traditions before gently waving away the cup he extended in my direction.

"You go ahead. I think Marcus and Brachan have returned. I'm going to go greet them."

I ran to the stables, a freedom I'd not felt in ages settling over me as I hurried to look for Marcus.

Ross was gone. He was never coming back. He could keep his secrets.

If happiness was within my grasp, I wasn't going to deny myself a moment longer.

I burst into the stables with what was probably a little too much enthusiasm before I forced myself to calm down and slowly walk over to Marcus, who'd only just turned toward the sound of my entry.

"Silva! God, it's good to see you."

He opened his arms to me as I walked toward him. I said nothing until I stood one small step away from him.

Rather than falling into his hug, I reached my palms up to his face to draw him near to me.

"Happy New Year, Marcus. I missed you so much."

He kept his eyes open as I pulled him toward me, his gaze conveying all of the questions and confusion I was certain he felt, but he didn't pull away from my kiss as I pressed my lips toward his.

It only took a moment for him to surrender to it, and as he wrapped me in his arms, I could hear the cheers of the others in the distance.

My only resolution for the new year would be joy—joy without guilt, without worry, and most importantly, without any more secrets.

CHAPTER 19

*O*f course he'd hoped she would be excited to see him. God knew how much he'd missed her while he was away. But however much he hoped, a greeting like what he received never crossed his mind. Marcus rarely allowed his imagination to run wild when it came to Silva. He cared about her too much to set himself up for the disappointment that would come if she was never able to give him hope.

But last night she'd given him hope, and it was more reason than ever before for him to have the conversation with Raudrich that he'd been putting off for far too long.

Marcus paused outside Raudrich and Laurel's bedchamber and listened for any embarrassing noises before knocking. The last thing he wanted to do was interrupt the two of them in bed—he'd done that once before, and it hadn't ended well for anyone involved.

When he heard nothing, he gave the door a soft knock and waited for one of them to answer.

To his surprise, Laurel answered. She immediately threw her arms around him.

"Marcus! Did Raudrich send you up here to comfort me? He

knows how maddening this latest manuscript has been. He also knows he's shit at saying the right thing to perk me up."

Marcus laughed as he wrapped his arms around his best friend. "He didn't, actually, but I'm happy to provide you with some encouragement, all the same."

Pulling away just enough to grasp onto Laurel's shoulders, Marcus looked down into her eyes and prepared to give her the speech he always used when Laurel needed an extra dose of encouragement. With her, tough love was always best. He suspected that's why Raudrich was so terrible at it—he could never bring himself to say a rude word to Laurel.

Marcus had known Laurel long enough to have no problem with it at all.

"Laurel, you listen to me. You pull this every single time you get about a quarter of the way through a manuscript. Finishing it is inevitable. Your wallowing in self-doubt and procrastination only delays the amount of time between now and the time when you're finished, which you know is the best feeling in the world. You're a grown-up, and grown-ups have jobs that they have to do whether they're feeling like it or not—regardless of whether the muse shows up to help them. Get over yourself and get in there and sit down to write. Don't come out of your room until you've met your word count goal for the day. If you just sit down and focus, it will go by much more quickly than you think."

He stopped and waited for Laurel to sort through her emotions once he finished. It was always the same. At first, her eyes would flash with anger, then her lip would tremble as if she might cry, and finally, with one big, deep, frustrated breath, she would sigh and nod before straightening up with resolve.

"You're right. Thank you. That's just what I needed. All right." She spun away from him. "Back to it I go."

He had to hurry to call out to her before she slammed the door his face. "Laurel, do you know where Raudrich is? I need to speak to him."

"I think he said something about fixing something or other in Nicol's room."

"Okay, I'll find him. Now, get back to work."

Laurel laughed as she closed the door to him.

———

*H*e could hear Raudrich banging around in their Master's bedchamber the moment he turned the corner to the long hallway that led to it.

Whatever it was, Marcus was certain it could've been easily fixed with magic, but he didn't blame Raudrich for wanting to work with his hands. As wonderful and convenient as their magic was, he often found that he gained more pleasure from doing hard work by hand.

He called out to Raudrich as he reached the open doorway. "Can I give you a hand with something?"

He stepped inside Nicol's room to find Raudrich bent over the scattered pieces of a chair as he worked to put it back together again.

"'Twould be a great help if ye hold this steady while I hammer this in."

Obligingly, Marcus went to grip the pieces together. "What happened to this?"

Raudrich shrugged and shook his head with concern. "I can only assume that he threw it." Raudrich paused and motioned to the wall of glass before continuing. "The window was cracked straight down. I had to fix it with magic. The whole room was a mess when he stormed away from the castle this morn. I doona know what caused it, but something sent him into a rage, and now he has left."

Marcus' mind immediately went to Freya. He would go to her as soon as the sun began to set tonight. He had no doubt that whatever had upset Nicol had something to do with her.

"I need to speak to you, Raudrich. Do you mind if I close the door so perhaps we won't be disturbed?"

When Raudrich nodded, Marcus set the pieces of the chair back down for just a moment so he could shut the bedchamber door.

"Do you think Machara can hear us up here?"

Raudrich shook his head. "A year ago, aye, she could have, but not weakened as she is now. 'Tis safe for ye to say whatever ye need to."

"Why have you waited so long to tell Silva about Ross, Raudrich?"

Raudrich sighed and set down his tools as he stood and began to pace the room. "I doona wish to hurt her, Marcus. Ye've seen how she has changed these past months here. She's healing from her grief. She enjoys it here. Once she learns that Ross still lives, she will go in search of him. I worry about what is in store for her when she finds him. If he wanted her, he wouldna have left her. I doona want her to have her heart broken twice."

The thought of Silva in any sort of pain made him miserable, but Silva wasn't as weak as Raudrich believed her to be. Even if Brachan was wrong, and Ross couldn't do anything to help them or Freya, Silva deserved to know the truth.

"Brachan has a theory about why Ross faked his own death."

"Does he?"

Marcus thought Raudrich couldn't have looked any more disinterested. He was certain that would change the moment he shared Brachan's suspicions.

"Yes. He believes that Ross was meant to be one of The Eight. That he knew it and that he fled to avoid his responsibility."

Raudrich stopped his pacing and moved to sit on the edge of Nicol's bed. "Do ye mean he believes 'tis Ross that should be here rather than me?"

Marcus shook his head. "No. He thinks I'm the one that's not supposed to be here. As accustomed as I've grown to my life here, I'm inclined to agree with him. Raudrich, I think it's time that I tell you what I've been up to these past few months. There may be a way for us to save Freya, but if Brachan is right, we will need Ross to do it."

———

*B*y nightfall, they'd come to an agreement. Ross had to be found. And Silva had to know the truth. They would tell her together, and she could choose if she wanted to be a part of their search. If not, they would do everything possible to shield her from him once they located him.

The choice would be hers, and finally, the truth would be out.

CHAPTER 20

I'd shocked Marcus. Even though he'd eagerly matched and returned my kiss, he'd not quite known how to react to me after I pulled away. We chatted for a few short moments before he introduced me to the young boy they'd brought back, Jimmie, but Marcus fumbled over his words the entire time. Once our kiss ended, I could barely get him to look me in the eye.

I was almost certain Jimmie would mean trouble for Liv. He was handsome and charismatic, and I was quite sure she wouldn't give him any option other than to fall in love with her. It was bound to mean chaos for all of us.

Shortly after I met Jimmie, the rest of the group became aware of Marcus and Brachan's return, and before long, all three men were so bombarded with greetings and questions that I decided to slip away for the night.

The next day, I hoped Marcus would seek me out so he could catch me up on everything they'd learned and so we could talk about our kiss. Instead, the entire day passed without me even bumping into him.

When he wasn't at dinner, I decided to go in search for him.

It came as no real surprise to me when I heard his voice upon entering the garden. Of course, he was with Freya.

"Marcus? Freya? Will I be intruding if I join you?"

Freya's voice drifted toward me as I neared them. "O'course not, lass. Marcus was just about to bid me goodnight. I believe he needs to speak with ye anyway."

As I stepped into their line of sight, Freya stood, her ghostly form rising effortlessly from the bench she floated above. She walked toward me, giving me a quick wink as she passed and rounded the corner to disappear to some other part of the garden.

"Should my ears have been burning?"

Marcus smiled before standing to come and meet me as I walked along one of the garden's many pathways.

"Maybe just a little. I'm sorry I didn't come to find you today. I had some things I needed to take care of that just wouldn't keep. I can't wait to visit with you alone, but Raudrich and I have something we need to discuss with you. Do you have a few minutes? He will probably already be waiting for us in the library if we head that way now."

Immediately, unease began to course through me. Little alarm bells started going off in my mind, warning me that all I'd vowed to leave behind only the night before was already coming back to haunt me. I didn't want any part of it.

"What's this about, Marcus?"

He stopped, and I could tell by the small, uncomfortable gesture he made with his nose that he didn't want to tell me. That was fine with me—I truly didn't want to know.

"I really think it's better if Raudrich and I talk to you about it together. He knew Ross. He knows more about this situation than I do."

I shook my head. I'd meant everything I'd felt so intensely the night before. Ross could keep his secrets. He was dead. They no longer had power over me. I wasn't curious. I didn't want them.

"No. I know Ross lied to me about Cagair. I know there are probably many other lies. I could see from how shocked Raudrich was to learn about Ross' magic that he would seek answers, and that's his choice to do so, but I want no part of it."

Marcus sighed and reached up to run a hand over his face before reaching for my hand.

"I understand that. I promise you, I do, but you need to know this. You'll want to."

It didn't matter what they were going to tell me. It wouldn't bring Ross back to me. In truth, I wasn't even sure I wanted him anymore. I'd give up my own limbs to get back the version of Ross I knew, but I no longer believed that the man I'd known had been real. I'd been in love with the great and powerful Oz, but underneath, he'd been someone very different. Someone who could lie to me to keep me captive in a time not my own—someone selfish enough to die and leave me.

I thought I was finished crying for Ross, but tears from somewhere deep inside me began to well up as I pulled away from Marcus' grip.

"No!" I knew I screamed a little too loudly. "No matter what you have learned about Ross, I don't want to hear a word of it. Not ever. All I want is to move on from him. Go and tell Raudrich that I don't ever want Ross' name mentioned around me again, and then, when you're ready to talk about literally anything else, come and find me."

I tore away from the garden and didn't look back or stop until the door to my cabin slammed shut behind me.

Once alone, I fell back against the door and cried for what I swore would be the last time.

"*W*here is she? Could ye not find her? I just saw Liv in the kitchens. I'm sure she will know where we can find Silva."

Marcus held up a hand to stop Raudrich, as he shook his head, his heart heavy and confused. Last night, he'd thought perhaps Silva's kiss meant she was ready to love again, but her reaction tonight had shown him that she was anything but.

Ross still had so much control over Silva's heart. There was still no room for him inside.

"She's not coming. She doesn't want to know."

Raudrich's thick brows pulled tightly together. "What do ye mean she doesna want to know? What did ye say to her?"

"I only told her that we needed to talk to her. She guessed it was about Ross. When I told her it was, she refused to come with me. She says that she never wants you to mention him around her again. She truly wants to leave him in the past."

"Why do ye look so devastated by that, Marcus? I can see that ye care for her. Shouldna ye be pleased that she is ready to move on?"

"Perhaps, but if she was so ready to move on, the very mention of him wouldn't have caused her to scream and run away in the other direction. She may think she's ready to move on, but she's nowhere near it."

Raudrich laughed and stood before walking over to him. "Then help her get ready, Marcus. Take yer time with her, aye, but I've always found that bravery is far more important than being ready. The verra fact that she says she wishes to move on takes more courage than ye can possibly know. The last thing ye should do is pull away from her, lad. If she doesna wish to speak of Ross, then we willna tell her. I shall begin searching for him on my own. I'll write to Sydney right away. She'll be happy to help, I'm certain. In the meantime, show her that ye are the man that Ross wasna. Show her that it shoulda been ye all along."

He desperately wanted to be that man for Silva. She occupied his every thought. She had for months.

"I don't see how we can shield this from her forever. Once we find him, she's bound to find out that he lives."

Raudrich smiled. "Then what are ye doing wasting yer time with me? Aye, I know 'tis likely that she will learn the truth, but if I were ye, rather than worrying about it, I'd be spending my time making sure that by the time she does find out, that her heart was truly and surely mine."

CHAPTER 21

"Silva, open the door. Do ye plan to sleep all day? What's the matter with ye? Are ye ill?"

Slowly, I opened my eyes and raised my groggy head from the pillow at the sound of Olivia's voice bellowing through the closed door.

My head felt heavy, my ears hurt, my throat was just about swollen shut. I was most definitely ill.

"Yes, actually, I believe I am."

There was a brief moment of silence before Liv's voice called out to me again.

"Then what are ye doing locking yer door? If ye are ill, ye need to let me in so I can care for ye."

Moving toward the lock, I turned it and stepped back so Olivia could enter. She looked me up and down and grimaced.

"Ye look frightening. Yer cabin even smells ill. How long have ye been feeling this way?"

I shrugged. "It must have come on sometime during the night. I knew I felt very stuffy when I went to sleep, but I assumed that was because I'd been crying."

She frowned and reached for my hand before thinking better of it. "Why were ye crying?"

"It doesn't matter. Can you go to the kitchen and get me some tea? And find Myla and ask her if she knows of any herbs I could use to perhaps feel a bit better? I know she's been studying them."

Olivia nodded and turned toward the door. "Aye, o'course. Did ye know there was a present outside yer door?"

I stepped toward the doorway to look outside. A dozen different colored roses from the garden were tied together with a letter. Smiling, I bent to pick it up as I hurried to open the letter.

Silva,

Join me for dinner tonight? I'll pick you up at 8:00.

Marcus

"*Well,* he's rather certain of himself, aye? He asked ye as if it were a true question, and then he just tells ye that he shall pick ye up regardless. Will ye go?"

I attempted to smell the roses, but only succeeded in sniffling. I couldn't smell a thing.

Still, I couldn't help but smile. Marcus had enjoyed our kiss, and he'd heard me when I told him I was ready to move on. Now, after what seemed like so many months since our little romance had begun, he was finally making a move.

"Yes. I'll feel better tonight if I have to will myself to health. Go and seek out Myla as quickly as you possibly can."

Olivia frowned. "Wouldna ye rather me get one of The Eight? They could use magic to heal ye."

The very thought seemed wasteful and frivolous. Magic was a

gift. The occasional sickness was entirely human. I could handle it without the use of such powers.

"Definitely not. I'll be better by dinner. I'm sure of it."

*A*ll the tea and herbs in the world weren't going to cure whatever ailed me. By the time night fell over the castle, I was ninety-nine percent sure that only time would do that—time I didn't have before Marcus was set to pick me up.

"Ye truly doona look so bad. Yer hair looks lovely pinned up as ye have it, and 'tis truly yer bonniest dress. I doona think he will notice the shade of yer nose."

The shade of my nose was firehouse red.

"Even if he was color blind—which I'm pretty sure he isn't—it wouldn't keep him from missing the constant stream of gunk dripping out of it."

I sniffled and sneezed and pressed my hanky to my face once more.

"Liv, I hate to do this, but will you go and find him and tell him I can't go? I definitely do not want him to see me like this."

As if summoned by my words, there was a rough knock on the door.

"Shit!" I collapsed onto the edge of the bed and waved Liv toward the door. "Send him away. Don't let him see me."

She smiled sympathetically at me, but I could see part of her was trying not to laugh.

"I know ye feel rotten, but ye truly think ye look worse than ye do, but aye, I will send him away if ye want me to."

Scooting to the far edge of the bed so Marcus couldn't see me once Liv cracked open the door, I listened on.

"Liv, good evening. Is your sister ready?"

Olivia sighed, and I saw her shoulders slump. She didn't want to let him down any more than I did.

"She desperately wanted to be ready, but I'm afraid she canna go with ye. She's quite ill."

"Is she really? Or does she just not want to go?"

Liv snorted, and I frowned.

"Ach, if ye saw her, ye'd know that she isna lying to ye."

"And you're her caretaker then?"

"Aye, I've been here all day, feeding her tea and Myla's herbs. Nothing's helped."

"You look tired yourself, Liv. I think it's time for you to take the night off. I'll take over from here."

My entire body tensed. Surely Liv had the common sense to know that I would simply die if she agreed to let him take care of me.

"I am rather tired."

I was going to kill her.

"I'm sure you are. They're just about to serve dinner in the dining hall. Run and get yourself something to eat. I promise you, I don't care what Silva looks like."

"That's what I told her, but she wouldna listen."

"Maybe she'll listen if I tell her myself."

And with that, he stepped inside while the rest of my face turned the same shade of red as my nose.

"Why didn't you send word this morning?"

"Because I just knew I was going to feel better by the time you got here."

"Myla's herbs aren't what you need, Silva. You need magic. I can have you feeling better in no time at all."

I shook my head defiantly. "No. I don't want to use magic to get over a little cold. It's wasteful."

I prepared myself for his rebuttal, but instead he simply nodded and moved toward the fire.

"Fine. I won't use magic, but I'm still going to take care of you. Take your hair down, change into some pajamas, and get into bed. I'll be back soon with everything I need."

CHAPTER 22

"Nicol and Freya are fighting now? That's the very last thing Freya needs. What if the stress of it causes her to fade even more quickly? I know she's tied to Machara, but haven't you noticed how Freya's moods seem to affect just how visible she is? When she's in a really good mood, she nearly glows. When she's down, her color is much flatter. It must mean that her own source of power has some strength too."

I was still sick. There was absolutely no doubt about that. But the steam bowl he'd made for me, along with the broth he'd whipped up in the castle's kitchen, had helped far more than the copious cups of tea Liv had supplied me with.

"Yes. Nicol left the castle yesterday morning. I was speaking to Freya about it before you came into the garden last night. She confronted him about her suspicions that he'd taken a lover. Nicol didn't take it well."

"I would think not. I don't blame Freya for wondering, but it's only further proof that Freya is as worried about her state as the rest of us. She should know how devoted he is to her."

"Deep down she does know that. It's exactly what you said—

she's frightened. She's always known that eventually Machara would be gone, and with it, so would she. But I think it has always seemed like that time was very far away. She can sense it creeping closer now."

I nodded as I scooted up in my bed so I could take another drink of broth. For hours while he cared for me, we talked about all he and Brachan learned while they were away. His kindness disarmed me and it didn't take long for me to forget how wretched I looked and just surrender to his capable care.

He pointed to the bowl I held up to my mouth.

"Finish that up and then turn around so that your head is at this end. I'll massage your head for a bit. I can tell it's hurting you."

My head was splitting from the pressure of my stuffed sinuses. A head massage sounded divine.

"How can you tell?"

"You keep squinting."

There wasn't much left in the bowl so I quickly threw it back and then crawled out of my covers so I could turn to lay my head in his lap. The moment his fingers wound their way into my hair, I sighed.

"That feels amazing. Is there anything you're not good at?"

He laughed and I opened my eyes to see his chin bobbing up and down in a yes.

"Plenty. I'm a terrible singer, and if there's ever a spider around, I am not the man you need to call. Insects terrify me."

I laughed, thinking of big, strong Marcus jumping at the sight of a spider. "You're joking."

His fingers moved to knead at my neck and I groaned. "I'm entirely serious."

I relaxed into him, allowing his fingers to work and roam over my scalp and neck. Slowly but surely, my headache began to dissolve. Just as I was nearing sleep, he spoke again.

"I believe the young man we brought back to the castle with us has a bit of a crush on your stepsister."

Sighing, I slowly lifted my head from his lap.

"I was afraid of that. What do you think about him?"

Marcus shrugged and stood to lift the blankets on the bed so that I could crawl back under them. I hesitated as I crawled inside and then scooted over just a bit before motioning for him to join me.

Smiling, he nodded before removing his shoes, slipping in next to me, and pulling me into his arms. My head moved to his chest with ease, and I smiled as he spoke into my hair.

"I'm not sure. I think he means well. He just still has a whole lot of growing up to do. He showed Brachan and me a great kindness, but he also lied, although I suspect it was out of necessity. The boy has no family. I believe he's been on his own for quite some time."

"I guess I'm going to have to let Liv make her own mistakes. I just hope she doesn't make any that will have her mother coming for my blood."

Marcus laughed and I trembled as his warm breath wafted down my spine.

"Is your stepmother that scary?"

I adore my father's wife, and it makes me so happy that she makes him happy, but I can't bear to think of her as my stepmother. "Please don't call her that. She's barely older than I am."

"What?" Marcus sounded appalled.

"My dad is quite a bit older than her. In fairness, he had me when he was sixteen, so it's not quite as creepy as it sounds."

I felt him nod against my head.

"Ah, I see. Silva." He hesitated, and I knew our conversation was about to take a more serious turn. "Can I ask you something?"

"Yes."

"What was that kiss on New Year's? Was it just tradition, or was it meant to tell me something? And please remember what I told you the first night you arrived here. You can't do or say anything that will take away my friendship. I hoped that the roses would convey my intentions, but I was going to ask what you wanted over dinner tonight."

Placing my palm on his chest, I lifted myself so I could look at him as I spoke. I'd wanted to be more than friends for far longer than I was comfortable admitting, but all he needed to know was that I was ready now.

"This year has been the most difficult of my life. For the longest time, I didn't want to feel anything other than my grief, because even though I was miserable, it kept me close to Ross. And later—when I did want to feel more than that soul-hollowing sadness—I doubted that I ever would again. The night of Laurel and Raudrich's wedding was the first time I realized that I still had some capacity to feel more than just numbness or sorrow. And that was before I really knew you. Your friendship has helped me believe that this could be my new home, but I'd be lying if I said my heart didn't speed up every time I looked at you."

I paused. I could see his breath catch as a vein in his neck began to visibly pulse more quickly. I smiled as I continued. "I'm not whole yet, Marcus. Not even close. I'll never be the same person I was before Ross died, but I'd like to discover the person I am now, and I'd like to do that with you if you'll let me. You'll have to tread carefully and take your time, but yes, that kiss was meant to tell you that I think I'm ready to see where things go."

Marcus smiled and leaned forward to give me one brief, soft, tender kiss before standing from the bed. "You've made my entire year, Silva. I've wanted you since the moment I saw you."

I giggled and snuggled back down into the blankets as he looked down at me.

"The year's only just started."

He nodded. "I know it has. You get some sleep. You need it. I'll come to check on you and bring you something to eat in the morning. If you're feeling any better, perhaps you can go with Brachan and me to Freya's gravesite tomorrow night."

For months, I'd been helping Marcus in his search to help Freya in whatever way I could. There was no way I was going to miss out on them finding out if there was still reason to hope or not.

"I'll feel better. I'm not letting you guys go without me."

CHAPTER 23

*N*o one breathed when Marcus and Brachan used their magic to open Freya's casket. She lay buried in a secluded corner of the castle grounds in a place where no one ever went, surrounded by trees. As long as she remained in the garden, where the people who loved her could see her and speak to her, her grave was no different than any other.

"I don't think I can look. If she's not...if she's..." Marcus couldn't even bring himself to say the words. I was quite certain I wouldn't be able to stomach the sight of Freya's skeleton, either, so I was grateful when Brachan reached out and placed a hand on Marcus' shoulder.

"Doona worry. I know what Freya means to ye. I'll look."

I reached for Marcus' hand, and we waited in silence as Brachan peered into her simple wooden casket in the moonlight.

"Christ, Nicol is a lucky man. She is even more gorgeous in the flesh."

Marcus nearly collapsed into me with relief as I moved to wrap both arms around him. "She's whole?"

Brachan smiled. "Aye, come and see, 'tis as I expected."

With the fear about what we might see inside the casket now gone, we walked over to look inside together.

"She looks like Snow White."

Marcus laughed as he nodded in agreement. "She really does. Now, let's close this up and bury her again before Nicol decides to make his way back to the castle. He'd kill us if he saw what we were doing."

I couldn't remember the last time I'd felt such pure hope. "It means we can save her."

I looked over at Marcus and Brachan to see them exchanging a concerning glance that I couldn't quite understand, but Marcus spoke before I had a chance to inquire what it was about.

"This is a start, at least. At least there is now a real chance."

arch 1652

*F*or at least the fifteenth time that day, I had to remind myself that I wasn't Olivia's mother, and I couldn't be as overbearing and protective as every instinct in my body was screaming at me to be.

After two and a half months of endless flirting at every meal, Jimmie had finally gathered up enough nerve to ask Olivia to accompany him on—hold your breath—a walk.

It wasn't that I was worried about Jimmie's behavior toward Olivia. I was actually quite impressed with everything that I'd seen from him. He was incredibly kind and attentive and seemed to be so grateful to Marcus and Brachan for bringing him here that his willingness to help with anything and everything that had to do with the two men was almost annoying.

No, Jimmie would be the perfect gentleman. I imagined the

most scandalous thing he would do to her was attempt to hold her hand, and I actually highly doubted that he would even work up the nerve to do that. Instead, I was worried about Olivia.

I remembered all too well what it felt like to be twenty, and Olivia was so much more green than I'd ever dreamed of being. It was too easy to get swept up in any emotion that made you feel alive at that age. It wouldn't take much for her to fall head over heels for just about anyone.

"A walk, Silva! 'Tis what men ask lassies to do when they mean to court them. I know he likes me. I've kenned that for months now, but I dinna think he ever intended to do anything about it. Are ye sure I look all right?"

I knew better than to say what I actually thought. She looked rather ridiculous. She had on her best dress, one so full on the bottom that it would drag the ground gathering up leaves like a vacuum cleaner. But she insisted that she felt most beautiful in this dress above all others and so I simply smiled and pulled her into a hug.

"You look beautiful." I hesitated, but then decide I couldn't help just saying one tiny thing. "Liv…"

She immediately held up a hand to stop me. "Only say something if ye intend to do so as my sister."

I could do that. I could say exactly what I wanted to, but in a sisterly way, surely.

"That's exactly what I want to do. All I was going to say is that you must remember that you are the most important person in the relationship, okay? This early on, you are the only person you should worry about. You're trying to figure out if he would add any value to your life, not trying to convince him of the value you would bring to his—that should already be apparent. You're test-driving the car, not him, okay?"

She scrunched her brows together and looked at me like I'd just sprouted another eye. "What are ye talking about? I couldna make sense of any of that, but it all sounds rather self-important."

Admittedly, it was, but I'd found that at least for the first few months of a relationship, selfishness was vital.

I sighed and tried to swallow the panic that rose up any time I thought about Olivia and love. "All I'm saying is, don't get swept away. Don't lose your head, okay?"

Olivia laughed and pulled me into a hug that reeked of sympathy. "Have ye considered that mayhap ye hang on to yer own head a little too tightly, Silva? Marcus has been saintlike in his patience with ye. Ye already know what a good man he is, but ye are keeping him at a distance all the same."

I didn't see it that way at all. "We're just taking our time, Liv. Neither one of us is in any hurry."

She pulled away and crossed her arms at me. "Yer certainly not, but I promise ye he's ready to repeat the events ye shared with him near on a year ago."

I blushed. "Hey now, who is trying to give whom advice here? You're the one about to go out on your very first date."

"Ye are attempting to give advice, but I doona need it. The reason ye are so worried about me losing my head is because ye know ye are far more prone to such behavior than I am. I know I'm young, but I'm more sensible than ye've ever believed me to be. Open yer heart just a little. Have a bit of fun. Lose yer head. 'Tis my advice to ye."

There was a knock on Liv's cabin door. Her date had arrived.

As I watched her leave, I couldn't help but feel like I'd just been schooled by my little sister, rather than the other way around.

ay 1652

ormally, journaling helped him. He cherished the way putting his thoughts down on paper helped things become more clear, but lately even that did nothing to relieve the stress that seemed to be mounting in everyone around the castle.

Nicol had been away for months. No one knew where he'd gone, but every few weeks they would receive a letter letting them know he was alive. His absence had sent Machara into a tailspin. While their captive faerie wasn't truly capable of love, every horrible thing she'd ever done was out of her obsession with Nicol. The fact that she could no longer sense him enraged her. As she raged, she weakened, and with her failing, Freya was now only visible for a few nights each week. Once she'd even been gone for three whole nights, and everyone in the castle had begun to despair that she was truly gone.

It would kill Nicol if he returned to find that Freya had gone to meet her final death without him being able to say goodbye.

To make matters worse, their continued search for anyone with powers stronger than their own—including Ross—had been unfruitful. Even Raudrich, who'd reached out to Sydney for help in the twenty-first century, had turned up nothing. She'd made the trip to Morna and Jerry's to ask for the old witch's help, only to find that they'd gone on an extended vacation to Australia and wouldn't be back until September.

Marcus sighed as he threw his quill across the old library before standing to run his hands over his face. He needed a shift, something to give him hope that things were capable of changing.

Even his relationship with Silva seemed to be at a standstill. He was crazy about her. Every day, she took ownership of a bit more of his heart, but he was under no illusion that he'd been so successful in laying claim to hers.

They spent time together every day. They would kiss and cuddle and laugh, but there was something about the way she held herself around him that told him she wasn't ready for more. Each night, he would bid her goodnight and retreat back to his room inside the castle.

His dreams were filled with his need to bury himself inside her.

"You look like hell."

Marcus pulled his hands away from his face to see Laurel enter the library. He opened his arms to her on reflex.

"I feel like hell. This has not been the best of weeks."

He relaxed a little as his best friend's arms wove around him and she squeezed tight.

"It's been a stressful few months, and it's time for you to tell me what's been going on."

He was certain she meant with Silva.

"Laurel, you know I love you, but I just don't feel comfortable discussing my girlfriend with you. You two have become quite good friends, too. It just doesn't seem right."

Laurel stepped away and moved to sit down at the table next to his journal. He hurried to slam it shut.

"I don't mean with you and Silva. I want to know what you, Brachan, and my husband have been trying to do these last few months. For the life of me, I will never understand why everyone sees the need to be so secretive around here. And why do you guys never involve the only people that every history book written about this place says will be the ones to end this—the women?"

Marcus shuddered at Laurel's assumption.

"Is that what you think I'm trying to do? It has never been my intention to be secretive. I just don't know if what we're trying to do is ever going to be possible, and I didn't want to get anyone's hopes up until I knew for sure if it was."

Laurel said nothing as she stared him down. He knew she wasn't going to let him out of her sight without a thorough explanation.

"I'm trying to save Freya."

Still, Laurel said nothing.

"We've learned that it might be possible. If we can find someone with druid power far stronger than any of our own."

Marcus could see the moment Laurel's wheels began to spin in her mind. It instantly made him wonder why he'd not been speaking with her about this all along.

"Are you saying that it's possible for someone like you guys to possess enough power that they could break Freya's tie to Machara before Machara is actually defeated?"

He sighed and collapsed into the chair next to Laurel's. "No. But if he was here at the moment Machara was defeated, he could free Freya then."

Laurel bit at her lower lip as she nodded.

"So, all of this is moot until each of us nine women have played our part?"

He nodded. "Yes, and I have no idea what to do about it. I guess I keep hoping that if we find a druid with enough power, he will know of a loophole around it—that he will be able to free Freya before she disappears into nothing even if the remaining women haven't yet played their part in Machara's demise."

Laurel made a clucking noise with her tongue as she drummed her fingers on the table in thought before speaking. "How likely is that?"

"Not very."

"So what has to happen? Let's talk it through."

He smiled at Laurel's matter-of-fact attitude about it all. "I don't know. We know that nine women have to defeat Machara, but there's no way for us to know who they are. Obviously we know two of them were you and Kate, but who else? I'm afraid that if we use magic to find them, it will ruin everything. It has to be mortal women—we can't interfere with magic. I guess we just have to wait until seven more women show up here."

Laurel shook her head and looked at him with an expression he recognized keenly as disappointment.

"Six more women. Surely, you've already decided that Silva is one of us. But that's beside the point right now. What if this druid —whenever you find him—can't free Freya without Machara being defeated? It could take another decade for six more women to show up here. Freya—if recent weeks are any indication—doesn't have that kind of time. We have to figure out another way."

He appreciated Laurel's determination, but as far as he could see, their hands were tied.

"I wish there was one, but I already told you, we can't use magic."

Laurel smiled and pushed herself away from the table. "We don't need magic, Marcus. Don't you remember how much Kate studied all of this before she came here? She was able to figure out that we were both supposed to be here by the clues in all that she found to read."

"I've read every book in this library. Nothing has helped."

Laurel shook her head in dismay. "Obviously. These books wouldn't help, would they? How would the books written in this time give clues about the women who are supposed to come here in the future? The answer is they wouldn't. We need the books from the future. The ones Kate read and studied at my apartment."

"And how do you suggest we go about getting those?"

Laurel smiled. "Isn't it obvious? It's time for you to make a trip back to Boston."

CHAPTER 25

"*H*as the gardenia angered ye, or is there something else that troubles ye?"

I jumped at the sound of Freya's voice behind me. Dropping the small set of shears in my hands, I turned toward her voice and held back the tears that threatened to spill at the sight of her.

"Ach, I can tell by yer face that it has been some time again, aye? How long was I gone this time?"

Brushing the soil from my hands, I stood and followed her over to one of the garden's many benches.

"Just two nights this time. Still too long."

"Aye. If only we had known such an extended absence from Nicol would weaken Machara so. Mayhap we should have sent him away a long time ago."

I frowned as I lowered myself next to her. "Don't say that. No one is ready for you to go."

She smiled sadly. "O'course not. I am not ready for it, either, but my time shoulda been the moment Machara killed me."

I desperately wanted to tell her what we were trying to do for her. Part of me believed that if we could just give her some hope it might allow her to hang on, but I knew how dangerous false hope could be. So I said nothing. It didn't take long for her to change the subject.

"What is on yer mind, lass? I doona believe 'twas me ye were thinking of when I spotted ye."

There was no reason to lie to her. I knew if anyone could give me advice, it was Freya. She was the castle's unofficial shrink.

"I think I'm allowing my fear to screw up something really special."

Freya didn't miss a beat. "Ye mean with Marcus?"

"Yes."

She reached out to lay her hand upon my own, but I felt nothing as I watched her ghostly hand lower to mine.

"I've seen the way he looks at ye. I've seen the way the two of ye are together, and I see nothing amiss. Just what is it that ye believe ye are destroying?"

I sighed as I thought back on each night Marcus dutifully left my cabin, never asking or pushing me to let him stay. I wanted him to. My dreams each night after he left were indication of that, but something stopped me every time I thought about pulling him back inside with me.

"It's been months, Freya. Months. And we've not been…" I hesitated, unsure of whether such conversation would make her uncomfortable.

"Ye havena tupped?"

I laughed at her frankness. "Well…yes, exactly. It's not him. I feel quite sure he would have done so anytime, but I've been pretty clearly closed off to it."

Freya smiled and shifted so she could look at me straight on. "I doona pretend to know much of such matters. Nicol is the only man I've ever been with, and it has been so long since I felt his touch, I am not so sure I remember what 'tis like. But it seems only natural to me that ye would be hesitant to be with another after losing yer husband."

I looked down as I spoke. "But you see, Marcus and I actually have already been together."

"Aye."

I jerked my head up in surprise. "You know?"

She laughed and shook her head. "Doona worry. Marcus said nothing, but ye are the woman from the night of Raudrich and Laurel's wedding, aye?"

"Yes. So you see why I'm so confused. I have dreamt about our night together more times than I care to admit. Why, then, am I so hesitant to repeat something that's already been done?"

Freya lowered her chin and looked up at me from underneath her lashes as if to say that it should've been blindingly obvious to me.

"Ye dinna love Marcus then, but ye are deeply in love with him now."

I knew she was right. I covered my face with my hands and groaned.

"What are ye thinking, lass?"

"It feels so different than before, Freya."

Her gaze was entirely patient as she gently prodded me into telling her more. "How do ye mean?"

"Before Ross came into my life, I was very practical in relationships. I took my time. I took care of myself. I always preferred it if the man was far more into me than I was him. I dated guys, but I never loved any of them. Ross changed all that.

"In a single instant, all of my resolve went out the window. He consumed me, and I was happy to let him do so. I loved him quickly and deeply, in a way that always felt dangerous, but I was powerless to stop myself from falling for him. It was as if in the course of a month, the person I'd been before Ross was gone. His love changed me that quickly. And when he left me, it shattered everything."

I realized as I finished that it was at least some progress that I didn't break down in tears when I spoke about him. It was the first time since the new year that I'd mentioned his name.

"And how is this different with Marcus? I can see ye are figuring this out on yer own as ye speak of it. Keep going, lass."

I laughed and furrowed my brows suspiciously at her. "Are you sure you're not secretly some twenty-first century therapist?"

She shook her head, obviously confused. "I doona know what that is, but aye, I'm quite sure. Now, go on. How is it different?"

"He hasn't swept me off my feet, Freya. I don't feel like a different person from having known him. If anything, I feel like I've become just a little bit more of who I am. I don't need him to get through the day, but I enjoy my days so much more when he's around. Everything about this is so much gentler than before. It's like a warm breeze that's slowly warming me through, not a giant tsunami intent on sweeping me away."

Freya snorted—something I'd never heard her do. I was actually surprised to learn that she was capable of making such a noise since she didn't have an actual nose for air to pull through.

"I doona know about ye, lass, but all of that sounds much more appealing than what ye described before."

It felt more appealing, too. It wasn't intense. It didn't overwhelm me. But there was an ease and natural build to my relationship with Marcus that felt so much more real.

"It is."

Freya nodded, knowingly. "And that 'tis precisely why it frightens ye. I doona believe ye are near ruining things with Marcus. He's a patient man, and I am fair certain he feels just the same way ye do, but it might make ye both feel better if ye share with him what ye just told me."

For weeks, all of this had been building. She was right.

It was time to tell Marcus how I really felt. It was time to let him into my heart.

*E*ven after all these months, the only time I'd ever stepped foot in Marcus' bedroom was the night of the wedding. We spent time in the garden or wandering the castle grounds. We would sit in the library or by the fire in my cabin, but I never dared venture into his room. I suppose we both knew what it would mean when I did.

We had no plans this evening so I hoped as I knocked gently on his door that he wasn't already sleeping. It took him no time at all to answer.

His eyes widened as he looked down at me. "Silva." He smiled and my nerves relaxed just a little. "Do you...do you want to come in?"

I nodded and stepped inside.

The entire room smelled like him—like the modern aftershave he had Sydney send along with the various modern supplies she sent monthly for us modern residents. It had quickly become one of my favorite scents in the world.

"I need to tell you something."

---

*F*inally, she was in his room once again. The sight of her standing near his bed flooded his mind with memories of him pressing himself into her in the darkness of that night so long ago.

He wanted to take her in his arms and kiss her until she surrendered to him. He wanted to make her scream out his name and tremble beneath him. He wanted her to bite his shoulder as she came.

Was her presence in his room because she wanted that very same thing? Was that what she was here to tell him?

Of all the nights for her to come here, she couldn't have picked a worse one.

Laurel was right. If The Eight had been unable to find a solution for Machara's defeat in the past two decades, what made Marcus think the solution was ever going to be found in this century? The solution lay in the future—in his own time—and he knew it.

He had to leave for Boston, and he had to do it soon.

It was possible he would be gone for months.

It wouldn't be right for him to take Silva to his bed, to confess his love for her and then turn around and leave her alone for such a long period of time.

Better to keep things how they were—committed but casual—where they could go several days without seeing one another and it was fine.

He stilled as she told him she needed to tell him something, and after a breath to suppress his need for her, he hurried to interrupt. "I need to tell you something, as well. I'm leaving for Cagair Castle in the morning, and from there I'm traveling back to the twenty-first century, and then onto Boston. I'll be able to research things much more easily from there. I'm hoping I can find something that will help us save Freya."

Silva spun toward him, her expression as shocked as he knew it would be. "Is Brachan going with you? Surely you're not going alone. I know in the twenty-first century things are likely to be fine, but it's not safe for you to travel the length of Scotland alone."

He shook his head. With Paton still stuck in the land of the fae, they could only spare one member of The Eight without their powers weakening.

"No. I'm going alone. I have magic, remember? If I run into any trouble, I'll use it."

She stared at him, and he could see that she was holding back from saying what she truly thought.

"How long will you be gone?"

"Months, possibly. I'll not return until I've found a way to end all of this for everyone."

Her arms came around him in an instant, and it was all he could do not to lift her in his arms and carry her to his bed.

"I'll come with you then. I promised once that I'd never return to my time, but I'm not sure that matters so much anymore."

Panic seized him. Ross was in the twenty-first century, and Marcus intended to find him. He couldn't risk Silva coming and learning that her husband was still alive.

"You can't."

She pulled away from him, her head cocked to one side.

"Why? I have no real responsibility here. Liv will be fine without me. Give me one good reason why I can't go."

He didn't have a good answer for her. He'd never been good at lying. "It just wouldn't be a good idea, Silva."

He watched as her jaw clenched, and his stomach tightened uncomfortably. He could see where this conversation would lead. Everything was about to come undone.

"I'm not sure you can actually tell me that, Marcus. I'm not a prisoner here. I can go to the twenty-first century on my own if I want to. Maybe I will. Maybe I'm just feeling like a trip to Boston."

He sighed and closed his eyes. "Silva, I'm begging you to drop this. You know that I'd love to have you at my side, but there's a very good reason why you shouldn't come with me."

Silva threw her hands up in exasperation. "Then tell me what it is."

He exhaled and looked down at the stone floor. "You don't want to know. We tried to tell you, and you told me you never wanted to hear his name again."

He watched nervously as her face paled and her hands began to shake. Somehow, some part of her expected what he was going to say—even if she didn't realize it yet.

Her voice shook as she spoke. "I've changed my mind. I think you'd better tell me now."

"Silva…" Never had anything been so difficult for him to say. "There's a very good possibility that Ross might be alive."

CHAPTER 26

*N*o. *No. No. No. No. No. No.*

My mind repeated the word as I paced around Marcus' bedroom.

It wasn't possible.

I'd watched him die.

I'd watched his body burn as we placed it on the pyre.

I'd visited his grave once a week for months.

But just as quickly as my mind rejected Marcus' words, other thoughts began to appear—thoughts that made me wonder— thoughts that made me shake with rage that it just might be true.

I'd never been able to feel Ross after he was gone.

I'd always found it strange that an illness of the chest could take down someone so powerful.

And finally, the thought that made me know it was true, and it broke my heart all over again, was my memory of the promise Ross had so desperately wanted me to make: that I would never travel forward in time again.

He'd known about Cagair. He knew I could return to my old life easily.

He simply didn't want me to. And I could think of only one reason for that.

He was there.

He'd left me to return to his life before me.

He'd allowed me to believe he was dead so he could live without me in another time.

A cocktail of anger, heartbreak, and betrayal coursed through me as I sunk to the floor and began to sob.

"I'm so sorry, Silva. I should've told you anyway."

I leapt to my feet, still shaking and unsteady, but not wanting to be in Marcus' presence a minute longer.

"You think?"

I ground out the question as I headed to the door. I didn't need to hear his answer. I didn't want to see his face. All I wanted was to be alone.

"Silva, wait."

I held up a hand to stop him, but I didn't turn around as I swung open the door.

"No, Marcus. I just need to be alone. Don't come after me."

By some miracle, I was able to make it to my own bed before I started screaming.

Marcus didn't stop until he stood outside of Laurel and Raudrich's bedchamber. This time he didn't care what he interrupted. Raising his fist, he banged on the door as loudly as he could.

Raudrich's voice bellowed through the door. "Whoever 'tis better have a good reason to be disturbing us this late in the evening."

"It's Marcus. Silva knows. I'm leaving in the morning."

"Silva knows what?"

Marcus groaned at the sound of Olivia's voice approaching him from the hallway. Sighing, he faced her. She would find out eventually, and Silva needed someone. He knew she wouldn't let him inside, but maybe she'd let Olivia.

Olivia repeated herself as she came to a stop in front of him. "Silva knows what?"

"It's possible that Ross might still be alive."

He expected the young woman's eyes to bulge out of her head. Instead, he found himself impressed by her calmness.

"And ye knew this?"

He gave Olivia one quick nod before she quickly began to shake her head in disgust.

"Men are fools. Every one of ye. Where is she?"

"She ran off to her cabin."

"And where are ye leaving to in the morn?"

"I'm going back to my own time to search for some information."

She surprised him by ramming a finger deep into the center of his chest. "If ye go anywhere before Silva has a chance to deal with what she's just learned, I shall steal a horse from the stable, ride after ye, and break yer nose. Do ye understand me? I'm sure she is angry with ye, but she needs ye. If ye leave come morn, ye will be no better than Ross."

"Okay."

Olivia was suddenly bearing a disturbing resemblance to his late grandmother. She was the only other person on earth who'd ever been able to make him feel so small.

"So ye willna leave?"

"No. I'll wait a few days."

She patted him on the shoulder like he was a small child. "That's a good lad."

She walked off without another word. By the time Marcus turned to face Raudrich and Laurel's bedchamber once again, Raudrich stood in the door with both of his cheeks puffed out uncomfortably as if he was stifling a laugh.

Marcus stood silently as he waited for Olivia to disappear down the stairwell and out the main doors of the castle. The moment she was gone, Raudrich doubled over in laughter.

"Christ, man, Jimmie doesna understand what he's in for with that lass. She should be master of her own castle. She looks as innocent and daft as a wee lamb, but 'tis only a façade, is it not? She's wiser and tougher than she looks."

Marcus nodded in agreement. "Yes. I haven't been spoken to like that since my grandmother died. I'm pretty sure she bruised me."

Raudrich laughed again and clasped him on the shoulder as he stepped fully out into the hallway. "Now...I agree that ye should go to Boston. Laurel told me about yer conversation. How did Silva come to know the truth?"

"She wanted to come with me. So I told her."

"Ah. And ye intend to find Ross while ye are there?"

"Yes. Even if I didn't want to kill him, I would still need to find him. What if Brachan's right? If he's the one that can save Freya, I have to seek him out."

Raudrich watched him carefully for a moment before speaking again. "Silva will come around, Marcus. 'Tis good that she knows. In truth, I shoulda told her the moment she told me of his magic. I bear some responsibility in this chaos."

Marcus couldn't agree more. He closed his eyes as a heavy weariness pulled down over him.

Anger always made him tired. He wasn't angry at Silva, of course, but seeing the heartbreak wash over her face as she learned about Ross' betrayal had sent fury coursing through him.

"Yes, you do, but I understand why you didn't do it. I'm leaving in three days, and I'm not coming back until I know exactly what we have to do. This brotherhood—all of us bound to one another and this place—it's not how I'm meant to live my life forever. It's not how any of us are meant to live. It's time for this to end."

CHAPTER 27

I didn't hear Olivia enter the cabin. I only noticed her once she slipped into bed next to me and silently pulled me into her arms.

I allowed her to hold me for what felt like hours, although I suspected it was really closer to a handful of minutes before I pulled away and sat up in the candlelit room.

"You know?"

"Aye."

I suspected everyone in the castle knew by now. If they didn't, I imagined I would have had more than one person knocking down my door to check on me from the way I wailed and screamed for the better part of an hour.

It had been a necessary thing—a visceral reaction that enabled me to survive the soul-crushing betrayal I now felt. I honestly believe that if I hadn't allowed myself those moments to scream at the top of my lungs, my heart would've burst from the pain.

"How could he do it, Liv?" I choked on the words as tears spilled over my cheeks again.

When I looked into her eyes, I could see that she was crying, too.

"I doona know. There is not a reason on earth that could justify it, so no matter how it feels in this moment, ye must know ye are better off without him."

In time, I knew I would feel that way, but now, I hurt too much to know anything.

"I loved him."

"Ye still love him."

I nodded as I closed my eyes. "I do. I still love him, but I hate him just as much."

Liv reached for my hand and gently bent to kiss my palm. "Aye. I hate him, too. I canna wait to see him again so I can bloody his nose."

I allowed myself one soft chuckle at the image of small, petite Olivia hurling her fist toward Ross' perfect face.

"Liv, we're not ever seeing him again."

She reached for my chin and lifted my face so that I sat up a little straighter.

"Aye, we are. Once ye realize that 'tis not Marcus' fault and ye forgive him, we are going with him to the twenty-first century, and we are finding yer arse of a husband."

I wouldn't have been any more shocked if Olivia had railed back and bloodied my nose.

"You think I would go anywhere with Marcus after learning that he kept this from me?"

She narrowed her eyes. "And why precisely did he keep it from ye? Be honest. I've already heard the answer."

"I know what I told him, Liv, but this is different. He shouldn't have listened to me."

She shrugged. "Mayhap so, but can ye blame him for not wanting to tell ye? He cares for ye. Not only would he not wish to see ye hurt by such news, but he also wants ye to be his and his alone. He is not a stupid man. He knows that as long as ye know that Ross still lives, ye willna truly be his. He made a mistake, but ye woulda done the same. I'm almost certain of it."

Perhaps she was right. I knew how insistent I'd been the night I told him I didn't want to hear what he and Raudrich had to tell me. I also knew that I would never want to see him in the sort of pain that I felt now. I, too, would do just about anything to shield him from it.

"Okay, say I can get past what Marcus did. Why would I want to go after a man who literally moved to a different century to escape me? He doesn't want me. He didn't want me so much that he was willing to make everyone believe he'd died. I'm inclined to let him think that I still believe that."

The little bit of my voice that remained after my screaming session cracked, and Olivia sighed before crawling out of the bed to fetch us both some water.

"Ye may feel that way now, but ye willna feel that way forever. If Ross lives, ye are still married to him. And whether ye've decided to admit it to yerself or not yet, ye are in love with someone else. What if one day ye wish to marry Marcus? Ye couldna ever bring yerself to do so when ye know that Ross lives. There is now too much unfinished business between the two of ye. We have to go, Silva. We have to go and find him so ye can get the answers to the questions ye havena even had time to form yet. We have to go so ye can tell him goodbye."

"You keep saying 'we.' Even if I do decide to go, Liv, there's no way you're coming with me."

She crossed her arms and straightened up a little taller. "Aye, I am. 'Tis not even a question. Ye are the one who told me to keep my head with Jimmie. Going with ye will give me the perfect opportunity to do so. Jimmie is perilously close to asking me to marry him. I can see it in the way he looks at me when we take our walks in the evenings, and I am not ready for that yet. How can I be when I've seen so little of the world? I am going whether ye wish it or not. I shall use my time away from him to search my heart for an answer. I canna be more sensible than that. I'm doing precisely as ye advised me to do."

I couldn't argue with that. No matter how much I wanted to, I couldn't argue with any of it.

"Fine. We'll both go."

For the second time in my life, everything had suddenly changed in an instant, and I was no more ready for it than I had been the first time around.

CHAPTER 28

I woke the next morning with more clarity than I knew was possible for me. For so long, I felt as if I needed to stuff my grief for Ross inside a box, to leave it fully in the past, but I knew full well that's not how grief works. Grief changes, but it never really goes away. You don't move on from it. You simply learn to make room for it inside your heart. You learn to let the warmer bits of you take up more space until eventually you get back to a place where there's more joy than sorrow. But the sorrow is always there.

I knew this, but it had never been the way I dealt with my grief over Ross. I tried to leave him behind on the mountaintop in Allen territory. I tried to leave him behind by moving here. On New Year's Eve, I once again tried to put him behind me, but I never could. Why did I try to force something I knew wasn't natural while grieving?

I woke with the answer.

Some secret part of me I never allowed to have a voice had always suspected.

I knew from the way Ross didn't fight his illness with the same urgency I felt when he got sick.

I knew the first time I'd wanted him but couldn't feel his spirit with me after he died.

I knew the moment Raudrich told me about Cagair Castle.

I just didn't want to know it. It was too difficult a truth to accept —that the man I turned my life upside down for was a liar—that he was someone who asked me to sacrifice so much but could betray and abandon me so very easily.

As painful as it was, I woke up free. Ross didn't want me? That was fine. I most assuredly no longer wanted him.

But there was someone else who *did* want me, someone who I knew with every fiber of my being would never treat me like Ross had. And I wanted him as much as I'd ever wanted anything in my life.

Olivia was right. If Ross was alive, there was unfinished business between us. What I felt for Marcus was real. I wanted him in my life. I wanted him in my future. I owed it to both of us to get to a place where I really could let Ross go, but I didn't want to do that without knowing Marcus would be at my side when it was done.

It was time for me to tell him.

***

I took my time getting ready for breakfast. I knew everyone in the castle would be on guard with me, and I didn't want to appear fragile or hurt. I put on my favorite dress, took extra care with my hair, and pinched at my cheeks to give them some color.

When I walked into the dining hall, everyone scrambled to pretend they weren't stunned to see me.

"Good morning, Silva. Did ye sleep well?"

I watched as Kate slapped Maddock's arm as if to tell him to shut up.

I decided right then it was best to address the elephant in the room.

"I know that you all know. I'm fine. Just please don't act strange around me. It will only make it harder."

In unison, they all nodded as Marcus hesitantly pulled out the seat next to him. He still wasn't sure I would want to speak to him. As I approached, the tension in his jaw visibly relaxed.

"It's okay, Marcus. I'm not angry. Not at you, anyway."

He reached over to squeeze my hand as I sat down. "I'm sorry, all the same. I knew better than to keep it from you, but selfishly I didn't want you to know. I was worried it would change how you felt about things, and I'm..." He hesitated. "I'm crazy about you, Silva."

I looked at his yet-to-be-filled plate of food and then looked him in the eyes. "How hungry are you?"

He shook his head. "I'm not. I'm so angry with myself, I couldn't eat a bite."

"Will you come with me, then?"

I kept hold of his hand and stood, knowing he would follow me.

I waited until we were out in the hall before I turned to face him.

Any of the fear I felt about being intimate with him was now gone.

I wanted him—needed him. Now.

Gently, I reached up to cup either side of his face. "Marcus, Ross being alive changes nothing. I know I've kept you at a distance, and I'm sorry. You've been so patient and kind, but I..." I trailed off as my voice failed me again. When I tried to speak, it was strained and broken. "I'm in love with you. I...I know you may not be there yet, and that's okay. I just didn't want to wait a minute longer to tell you.

"You have to let me go with you to Boston. I have to find Ross. I have to speak with him, but I don't want to do that without you in my corner, without you knowing that it's you who now has my heart."

His lips crushed against mine as he backed me into the wall, his hands moving into my hair as I opened my mouth to him.

He kissed me until I was breathless before moving his lips to my ear.

"I have loved you for longer than you can possibly know. Please let me take you to my bed."

Marcus' bedroom was on the opposite side of the castle, but the basement pantry staircase was just around the corner.

Breathlessly, I shook my head and tore myself away from him, grabbing his hand to pull him along behind me.

"Your room is too far away."

Groaning, he yanked me toward him, spinning me so that I faced him once more before he lifted me into his arms. I straddled him as he kicked open the door and stepped into the darkness.

CHAPTER 29

*H*e nearly tripped twice in his haste to get me down the dark staircase, but with more grace than I would've been able to muster, he caught himself while still keeping a tight grip on my butt.

When we reached the bottom of the staircase, he lowered me to my feet just long enough to light the candles scattered in the darkness with a quick wave of his fingers. As the room illuminated, he turned toward me. My breath caught at the hunger in his eyes.

"Do you know how badly I've wanted to touch you? Do you have any idea how much you have tested my patience?"

I smiled at him as I reached for his arms. I was desperate to have him closer to me. I wanted his hands on me. I wanted to feel him everywhere.

"I know. You're a good man, Marcus."

He let out a noise that sounded more like a growl than anything else as his lips moved to suck and bite on my neck as I gasped for air.

When I yelped at one particularly hard suck, he raised his lips just long enough to say, "I don't think I can be a good man right now, Silva."

His words were nearly enough to make me come.

I shook my head wildly as his hand traveled downward to my breast, first cupping and then tugging at my nipple so roughly I cried out once more.

"I don't want you to be good anymore. I want you to take me however you need to. Right now, Marcus. I need..." I groaned as he dropped his hand and grasped in between my legs through the fabric of my dress. "I need you inside me."

The night we'd spent together during Raudrich and Laurel's wedding had been passionate and long, but he'd been very gentle with me. That wasn't what I wanted now. I needed to feel all of his pent-up sexual desire. I wanted him to lose himself as he plunged inside me. I wanted to take all he could give. I was ready for it. I needed it. There would be time for gentleness later.

"Silva, are you sure you want to do this here? I don't know..."

I silenced him by leaning forward to bite at his lower lip as I gripped his erection.

He shivered and jolted underneath the grip of my hand as he groaned and reached up to tear at the front of my gown. It ripped with ease. I laughed as my breasts sprung free.

"Did you use magic to do that?"

He grinned mischievously and leaned forward to quickly nibble at my ear. "Oh, Silva. I don't need magic to help me with this."

I leaned back into the wall and moaned as he bent his mouth to my breasts and sucked one of my nipples deep into his mouth.

While his tongue sent me into a frenzy, he moved his hands to pull down the rest of my gown until I stood before him naked.

I reached for the pin in his kilt, desperate for him to remove it so our bare skin could touch.

He could sense that I struggled with it and pulled away from me with a smile.

"They're the damnedest things. I hate them."

I watched intently as he removed the pin and began to pull at his kilt. I couldn't wait to see his erection spring free in front of me.

I already knew what he looked like—how impressive the sight was —but I couldn't wait to see it again.

"If it makes you feel any better about them, you look incredible in a kilt."

He laughed, and blessedly, the fabric finally dropped to the floor as he removed his linen shirt.

"It doesn't, but thank you."

I glanced down at him slowly, knowing he would see where my gaze fell. Slowly, I closed my eyes in anticipation.

"Take me, Marcus. Take me now."

He laughed again and I felt my center grow wet with anticipation.

"You've been so hesitant for so long. I never expected you to be like this."

I bit at my lower lip and narrowed my eyes at him.

"I'm full of surprises, Marcus."

He moved toward me, lifting me off the ground again as I wrapped my legs around him.

He kissed me—his tongue diving deep as he carried me to a wooden table in the corner of the small storeroom.

The moment he lowered me to the table, he plunged inside me, his mouth covering my own as I cried out in pleasure at the fullness of him.

"Oh, I've missed this!"

They were the last coherent thoughts my mind formed as I succumbed to his rhythm and the waves of pleasure that found us both.

---

*T*oo weak and sated to stand, Marcus cradled me in his arms as he bent to gather our clothing before exiting the basement.

He stood cautiously in the hallway, glancing back and forth to make sure the coast was clear before taking off toward his room at a speed that had my head bouncing up and down off his chest as I laughed hysterically the entire way.

By some miracle, we made it to his room unseen. Once there, he gently lay me down on his bed.

"Would you like a bath?"

I grinned. "Only if you're willing to lift me into it."

He turned away, and I noticed the smallest movement of his hands before the tub began to fill with steaming water from the bottom.

"I insist on lifting you into it. The others would chastise me for using magic this way, but I'm not waiting the time it would take to make us a bath by hand. I need you in my arms right now."

Moving to the bed, he lifted me once again and carried me to the large tub. Gently, he stood me in the water, keeping a grip on my arms as he stepped in behind me. Carefully, he pulled me against him, and we slipped down into the tub until I leaned back against his chest, the warm water causing me to sigh.

"God, the water feels good."

He gave me a little squeeze as he kissed the top of my head. "You feel good, Silva."

As the water relaxed us, we lay in silence until it began to cool.

Eventually, I twisted back to look at him. "When are we leaving?"

He sighed. I knew he had reservations about me seeing Ross again. I would just have to make certain that by the time that happened, there was no doubt in his mind about how much I belonged to him.

"Tomorrow, if you and Olivia are willing. The sooner we can find the information we need, the better."

As if on cue, Marcus' bedroom door burst open. I jumped at the noise, and then hurried to cover all of my bits and pieces. I looked up to see Olivia standing in the doorway, both her hands plastered over her eyes as she kicked the door shut with her foot.

"Doona worry. I'm not looking at ye. But ye are both mad if ye doona think everyone in this castle doesna know what ye are up to. Noise from the storage basement carries into the dining hall. Ye should have seen the blushes around the table."

CHAPTER 30

It took us a moment to recover from Olivia's sudden interruption and to process the news that everyone in the castle had been forced to listen to our lovemaking.

I gave my head a gentle shake to clear it before I responded to her. "Liv, just stay right there and keep your eyes covered. I can't talk to you while I'm naked. Let me get dressed."

I stood up in the tub and looked around the room for something to dry myself with.

Marcus was already on top of it and had stepped out beside me as he reached for a blanket to drape around me before doing the same for himself.

"Doona worry, Silva. I've no desire to see either one of ye. I'll not peep until ye have assured me 'tis safe to do so."

Marcus leaned forward and whispered in my ear. "I'm afraid you don't have anything to put on in here. I ripped your dress, remember?"

I looked up at the ceiling and groaned. "Shit." I paused and scrunched up my nose in Olivia's direction, although I knew she couldn't see my guilty expression. "Liv, do you mind running to my cabin and getting me something to wear? I'm afraid what I had on before is ruined."

She made a gagging sound as she nodded and fled the room. The moment she was gone, Marcus burst into laughter.

"Dinner should be fun tonight."

I covered my face with my hands. "I'm mortified."

Still laughing, he pulled me into a hug as he kissed the top of my head. "It was worth it though, wasn't it?"

I could still feel the aftershocks of my orgasm. I smiled as I allowed myself to lean into his chest. "Yes. It was most definitely worth it. I can live with a little embarrassment."

He pointed behind me at the door. "What do you think that's about? She must've been desperate to talk to burst in here like that."

I shrugged against him as my body began to dry and warm. "If I were to guess, I bet it has something to do with Jimmie."

The door flung open once more as I felt what was presumably a dress hit me in the back.

"My eyes are closed. Hurry and dress, Silva. I doona have much time, and I doona know what to do."

I stepped away from Marcus and hurried to dress myself. He did the same.

Once we were decent, I gave Olivia the all clear. "Okay, open your eyes and tell me what's going on."

She groaned and dramatically threw herself down into the nearest armchair as she covered her forehead with one of her hands. "I told Jimmie that I was leaving with ye, and now he wants me to meet him in the garden straight away."

I looked at her blankly, unsure of what she wanted me to say. "I'm sorry, Liv. I'm going to need a bit more information than that. What's wrong with meeting him in the garden? You two love to go on walks together."

She widened her eyes and leaned forward in her seat. "Doona ye see, Silva? I could see it in his eyes the moment I told him I was going away. He canna bear the thought of it. He means to ask me to marry him."

"Ohhh…" I drew the word out as Olivia's concern suddenly made much more sense to me. "And you're definitely not ready for that."

"O' course not!"

She screamed at me as the first trace of tears popped up in her eyes. I hurried to pull her into my arms.

"Take a deep breath, Olivia. If you don't want to marry him, if you're not ready, then you don't say yes. It's perfectly okay."

She shook in my arms. I'd never seen her so upset.

"But I doona want to lose him, Silva. I know 'tis not fair to him, but I doona know what I want, and until I do, I doona want to lose him."

I smiled as I hugged her. "You won't lose him, Liv. He's crazy about you, and marriage is a very big deal. It's okay to be selfish in this situation. Just be honest with him."

For the first time, Marcus' voice joined in from behind me. "For what it's worth, I agree with Silva. I don't think there's anything you could do to scare Jimmie off."

She pulled away, relief etched onto her face as she looked over my shoulder at Marcus. "Truly? Ye doona think so?"

Marcus nodded. "You have him wrapped around your finger, Liv. I guarantee you, you're safe."

She smiled and stepped toward the door, all of the heaviness from her expression now gone. "Then, I shall tell him the truth. Thank ye."

And with that she was gone, leaving us alone in Marcus' bedroom once again.

I spun to face him with a smile. "I have to say. It's a relief to see Olivia crack just a bit. She is wise for her age, but I needed a reminder that she really is still incredibly young."

"It's always easier for us to be wise when it comes to other people's situations. We all tend to lose our perspective when it pertains to us." He paused and wiggled his brows suspiciously. "Do you want to go and spy on them? There's a back door to the garden that only a few of us know about."

My better angels quickly rose up to voice how wrong it would be to eavesdrop, but it didn't take long for my curiosity to get the better of me. "They won't know we're there?"

He shook his head. "We will be as quiet as a mouse."

Convinced, I nodded excitedly. "Then, I'm definitely in. Let's go."

Olivia must have taken a moment to gather herself before meeting Jimmie because Marcus and I were already secretly situated in the garden before she walked inside.

If I hadn't known Olivia so well, I would've felt rotten, but it was precisely the sort of thing she would do to me if given the opportunity. In fact, I was certain that she had done something similar on more than one occasion.

The moment Olivia stepped into Jimmie's line of sight, he jumped up from the side of the fountain where he was sitting. I smiled sympathetically for him as I noticed his hands were shaking.

"Do ye know how beautiful ye are, Olivia?"

I didn't miss how she blushed at Jimmie's words. She might not know exactly what she wanted in her future yet, and she definitely wasn't ready for marriage, but she was still crazy about the besotted young man in front of her.

"No, but ye never cease trying to convince me."

Jimmie took one step forward, and I was quite afraid that I might start to cry. As if Marcus could feel my emotions start to rise up in my chest, he placed a gentle hand on my back as Jimmie spoke.

"Aye, until ye know it through and through, I willna stop. Even then, I canna promise ye anything. Lass, I've been thinking on what ye told me at breakfast. I think it a fine idea that ye should seek to see more of this country for a time, but I want ye to know just how badly I shall miss ye."

I could see in the way Olivia's shoulders tensed that she was getting ready to stop him, but before she could say a word, he held up his palm to stop her from speaking.

"No, Liv. Allow me to finish. I can see ye are frightened by what I might say, but ye are wrong. I only mean to tell ye this: I know that I want ye. I've seen more than I hope ye ever have to see. I've been through things I wouldna wish on my greatest enemy. I've had the opportunity to search this land and get to know myself in ways that ye have not. Ye deserve that. But once ye return, I need to know one way or the other, lass. Doona return here until ye can either accept all of me or turn me away. I am in love with ye, Olivia. I doona think 'tis wrong of me to wish to know where yer heart truly lies."

Whatever I had expected from the young man, it certainly hadn't been this. Like the woman he loved, Jimmie was wise beyond his years. I looked into Olivia's eyes as she stared at him, and I knew—if she wasn't in love with him before, she certainly was now.

She would take this time away from him, but when she returned, her heart would undoubtedly be his.

Surprisingly, despite their young age, I was at peace with it.

I couldn't see her ever finding a better match.

ne Week Later

he journey to Cagair was long, but not nearly as difficult thanks to Marcus' rather generous use of magic. I knew him well enough to know that had it only been him traveling, he would never have indulged in such a way, but he was intent on making certain that Liv and I were safe, warm, dry, and relatively comfortable the entire way there.

Olivia's excitement was bubbling over by the time we could see Cagair in the distance. The entire journey she'd badgered Marcus and me with questions about twenty-first century life and the wonders she was going to get to see and experience.

She would be useless in our search for information—all Olivia wanted to do was explore and marvel at all the new things that awaited her. That was just how I wanted it. While I knew we would eventually have to begin searching for Ross, I wasn't in any hurry to do so, and I didn't really ever want Olivia to see him. I was fairly certain she would keep her promise to bloody his nose if she ever did.

"Are you nervous to go back?"

I looked to my left toward Marcus' voice as he pulled back on his reins enough so that Olivia was riding a little bit ahead of us.

"Yes." I wouldn't lie to him. "But I also can't wait to enjoy some of the simple pleasures I've missed."

He smiled. "Me, too. I know we have to find a way to save Freya, and I will look endlessly until I do, but I think we've both earned a little bit of fun, as well."

"What are you looking forward to doing the most? What have you missed more than anything else?"

He waited for a long moment to answer me and I understood his hesitation. The world both Marcus and I were born in and the world in which we now called our home were like two entirely different planets. It was difficult to pick just one thing.

"Hmm…" He scrunched his nose and cocked his head to the side. "I'm really looking forward to not using magic for awhile, strangely enough. Almost everything that I use magic for in this time is done with very little effort in ours. I'm ready to give it a rest."

I'd always gotten the impression that Marcus quite enjoyed his newfound gift. His statement gave me pause.

"Won't you miss it?"

While we all supposed Marcus' powers would remain in the twenty-first century, he'd promised all of the members of The Eight that he wouldn't use them once we went forward. Magic from one drained power from the others, and at such a great distance, they couldn't afford for their powers to weaken enough to give Machara strength.

Marcus didn't hesitate to answer. "Not at all."

"Really?"

"Really. I've accepted my magic, but I'm not sure I'll ever feel like myself with it. It wouldn't be hard for me to walk away from it."

When I said nothing, he directed the subject back to me. "What about you, Silva? What are you most excited about? You've been gone for far longer than I have."

"Honestly, I can't wait to sit and binge a whole day of rom-com movies with Olivia. I can just picture how pure her joy will be at experiencing them. I can't wait for it."

He laughed and pulled his horse to a stop to dismount as we neared the pathway to the castle.

"Then, that's what we should do tomorrow. It's been a long trip, and from what Raudrich said, Sydney will be a lot to handle for the first little bit. I think we all need a few days of rest before we really dive in and get to work around here."

Nothing sounded better to me.

Dismounting, I called ahead to Olivia. "Wait up for us, Liv."

She waited, but I could see how much it tried her patience to do so. She was bouncing up and down with excitement. When we reached her, we walked forward to the stables together.

I wasn't a bit surprised to see Sydney standing outside waiting for us.

"You're here! Everyone is so excited!"

She turned away from us just long enough to call after two workers in the stables who quickly came out to see to our horses. The moment they were led away, she waved us in for a big group hug.

"Okay, I know you all must be exhausted, so I'm going to fill you in on everything as quickly as I can. The plans have changed in the past week since you headed in this direction. The moment I received Raudrich's letter detailing how you all intended to go to Boston, I tore it up and said hogwash with all of that. It would be far too complicated since Morna is out of touch for the time being."

I was increasingly curious about this Morna person so many of them spoke of. I sincerely hoped that at some point I would have the opportunity to meet her.

Marcus spoke up as Liv and I attempted to pull ourselves out of the team huddle. "So, we're not going to Boston?"

Sydney righted herself while shaking her head and turning to walk toward the side of the castle. Instinctively, we all followed along.

"No. None of you have passports. While we dabble in magic, we're not really running a criminal enterprise here, so without Morna, none of us have the slightest clue how to forge one for you. Instead, Gillian and Orick have flown to Boston where they will collect everything that Kate left behind in Laurel's apartment relating to The Isle."

Marcus cast me a quick, wide-eyed glance as if to tell me that Raudrich had definitely been correct about Sydney's whirlwind personality.

"How will they get into her apartment?"

Sydney threw a quick smile over her shoulder at us as she continued to march on. "Kate left her keys to the place here since we live in the twenty-first century most of the time, in case anyone ever needed to go back there. Gillian and Orick have been at Laurel's old place for several days and are flying back tomorrow."

She suddenly stopped in front of an oddly shaped door at the side of the castle before she faced us and continued speaking. "In the meantime, I ordered every book and video I could find about The Isle online, and I already have them set up in a study room that is exclusively for your use while you are here. We've also set up three rooms, but you're free to..." She paused and waved a finger between Marcus and me, "...combine rooms if you like. Just let me know if that's what you'd like to do so we can open up the extra room to other guests."

Sydney stopped and looked at Olivia straight on to address her. "If you'd like, once you have the opportunity to explore and enjoy things for a few days, we thought we might offer you a small job while you're here. We're an inn, you see, and we need someone to work the front desk for a few hours each afternoon."

Olivia beamed. "A job? Truly?"

Sydney smiled. "Yes, and we will pay you and everything."

Olivia turned bewildered eyes on me. "I've never had my own money before."

I mouthed the words *thank you* to Sydney before answering. "Then, it's well past time for you to do so. Once you get some saved, I'll even take you shopping for some special things you can bring back with us when we go home."

Olivia looked as if she might cry. Before she had the chance, Sydney started up again.

"I also went shopping for all of you. There's a small, but livable, selection of clothes and toiletries in each of your rooms. I hope they suit your tastes."

I reached out to squeeze Sydney's arm. She must have been working around the clock to prepare for us. We all couldn't have been more grateful.

"It will be perfect."

She clapped her hands together excitedly. "Great. Are you ready to travel through time?"

She pushed open the door to the strange stairwell that led to what looked like just another wall at the bottom.

It took Olivia all of three seconds to take off at a sprint toward the bricks.

She didn't flinch as she stepped through them and disappeared.

---

*G*lasgow, Scotland - Present Day

. . .

*W*as he having a heart attack? The pain in his chest never left him, but why was it suddenly worse?

He slumped to the ground in his shabby apartment as realization hit him.

It was her.

She was here, and the pain of feeling her once again was most certainly more than he would be able to bear.

uly

ension radiated off Marcus as he parallel parked our tiny rental into the tight space outside of the professor's home. I waited until he turned off the engine and grabbed the door handle before reaching for him.

"Breathe, babe. I know you're stressed. I know it's been a frustrating few months. But let's go in with an open mind, okay? It's kind of this man to invite us to his home."

Marcus sighed and leaned his head back against the headrest. "The man is a quack. He invited us to his home because after years of every professional in his field ridiculing his work as pure fantasy, someone has taken him seriously. He's flattered."

"Marcus." I crossed my arms until he lifted his head to look at me. "You are a black man born in Boston, Massachusetts in the twenty-first century who is now a member of a druid sect that is bound to protect an isolated island from the powers of a vengeful faerie in the seventeenth century, and you're calling this man a quack because he believes the old legends about The Isle? Please tell me you realize how crazy that makes you sound."

He stared at me a long moment before he laughed and shook his head as he leaned against the steering wheel.

I knew how stressed he was. Our inquiries into Ross' whereabouts had come up empty. And even after months of researching, reading, and traveling to libraries and universities, we still knew nothing that would help us save Freya. He was worried that we were running out of time.

I was worried too, but I knew that giving up meant certain failure.

"You're right."

Of course I was. In my mind, our discovery of the twenty-five-year-old documentary by the then student—now professor of Scottish legends and lore—Dougal Anderson was the exact break we'd needed in our search.

While much of what the documentary alleged didn't line up with the reality we knew on The Isle, it was evident that the passionate young creator of the film believed that all legends hold at least some basis in truth. That—to me anyway—was reason enough for us to reach out to him. To my everlasting gratitude, he'd promptly replied. After a week of correspondence in which he'd recommended another dozen readings for us, he'd invited us to his home.

"Besides," I said, as I leaned over to kiss his cheek, "once we're done here, we get to go and enjoy the fancy dinner we reserved. And you know what else?" I turned his face toward me as I kissed him. "I brought a dress that's going to knock your socks off."

He laughed into my mouth as he answered me. "Everything you wear does that."

I pulled away and shook my head dismissively. "You're sweet, but you haven't seen this yet. You're not going to be able to keep your hands off me on the drive back to Cagair tonight."

He groaned and pulled me in to kiss me just as there was a quick rap of knuckles on Marcus' window.

We both jumped and turned to look over at the most amazing looking man I'd ever seen.

Professor Anderson couldn't have been much taller than four feet six inches. He wore gray slacks with a bright pink and green plaid button-up shirt underneath a purple vest. He looked like someone from an old-fashioned ice cream parlor.

His snow-white hair was thick and messy on top of his head and his glasses magnified his shockingly blue eyes to three times their normal size.

He grinned widely as Marcus moved to roll down the window.

I knew right away that I would like him.

"Ye've made it. Come in, the both of ye. I've the kettle on and biscuits baked."

He didn't wait for us to answer him as he turned and marched back into his home.

I couldn't wait to see inside. With such a vibrant personality, it was bound to be eccentric.

"Well," Marcus laughed as he opened the door to step out into the unusually hot day,

"at least he's excited we're here."

Eager to begin our conversation, I stepped out of the car and all but ran into the old man's home.

It did not disappoint.

"Whatever led ye to believe that 'twas years after the arrival of the first woman that tested Machara before the last one arrived?"

I glanced over at Marcus as Dougal questioned us. I'd just finished explaining to him that we were doing our own research for a future book we hoped to write on the subject and that we were having difficulty piecing together a timeline of events. I told him that we knew it was thought to have taken a very long time, but we couldn't know for sure. I had hoped that if the professor could give us a more definite time frame, it would narrow down our search, and we could begin to look for other clues in books about the women who might arrive after me on The Isle. But Dougal's question gave me pause. Had we actually ever read anything to that effect, or had that been our blind assumption?

I knew we were trying to speed things up by searching books for clues about who the other women might be, but was it possible that things were supposed to move quickly after Laurel's arrival, all along?

"I…" I opened my mouth to answer him, but found that I had no good answer. I shrugged, feeling bewildered and foolish. "I don't know."

Dougal eyed me suspiciously from over the top of his mug as he sipped on his fourth cup of tea. Slowly, he lowered it as he spoke. "Unfortunately, legends are never history. Was Machara truly from the world of the fae?" He paused and pulled his lips to one side. "Most would say no. Were the men who lived there truly druids? Mayhap so, but if they were, 'tis likely they had no real power."

I looked over at Marcus and did my best to suppress a grin. The corner of his mouth was twitching. Even though he wasn't nearly as attached to his magic as the other members of The Eight, I could see that part of him wanted to show the old professor just how much magic he actually possessed, but sensibly, he refrained and gave me the slightest nod as his way of encouraging me to continue.

"What do you believe truly happened there?"

"The Isle is still such a place of mystery. Few like to visit there. That alone is proof that the legends carried enough truth to be passed down through the centuries. I believe there was evil there, but all one needs to do is look around this world as it is now to see that just as much evil resides in the physical realm as it does in the supernatural. I believe there were eight men who banded together to stop whatever 'twas that threatened terror on The Isle. And most importantly, I believe 'twas the wisdom of the women in these men's lives that ultimately restored peace to this secretive spot in Scotland."

"But you don't believe that it took years for these women to come together on The Isle?"

He shook his head. "No. None of my research into the legend supports this theory. In fact, I've found multiple writings that detail that after the first two women married into the clan, the rest arrived at the castle within a year."

My heart sped up as hope filled me. It wouldn't be long before I'd been at the castle a year, which meant that it was plausible that we would succeed in finding the remaining women needed to defeat Machara and hopefully save Freya's life.

For the first time in over an hour, Marcus leaned forward to speak. His voice was filled with excitement. "Have you come across anything that tells where these other women came from?"

He shook his head. "I doona know. There is little written about any of them, and I believe 'tis because it all ended rather quickly after they came together on The Isle. And this…" He paused as if he was unsure if he should finish his thought. When I nodded him on, he continued. "There is no evidence for this—'tis just my belief based on my knowledge of the legends. I believe all the women were somehow connected to the first. There is a common thread between them—something that tied them all together."

e skipped our fancy dinner. Marcus and I were both so excited to have some new piece of information to run with that all we wanted to do after we bid the old professor goodbye was get back to Cagair Castle so that we could settle in for a brainstorming session in the room Sydney had set aside for our study.

The long drive back went quickly as some of the stress we'd both been carrying for weeks seemed to have abated a little by Dougal's words. If he was correct—if all the women needed to defeat Machara came together within a year—then it wasn't a stretch to assume that despite our frustration now, we would eventually succeed in finding them.

"Do you think Olivia will still be up?" Marcus asked as he pulled the car to a stop in front of the castle that truly had begun to feel like a temporary home of sorts after so many months.

I nodded, playfully. "Oh yeah. I haven't been able to pull her away from Netflix. She's definitely sitting there with a bowl full of popcorn and a bottle of cherry soda binge-watching like crazy."

Marcus laughed. "I think she's already put on a good *freshman fifteen.*"

I gave him a quick disapproving look. "Maybe so, but at least she could afford to do so. But Marcus, never, ever say that to her."

He turned shocked eyes on me. "You do remember that my best friends are women, right? I know better than to ever say anything to a woman about her weight. What's she watching now?"

I smiled hesitantly as I braced for Marcus' inevitable blowback. "She's deep into season five of *Friends.*"

He frowned and rolled his eyes, disapprovingly, as I'd known he would. "I wouldn't think that a girl born in seventeenth century Scotland would see the humor in *Friends.*"

I sighed. "Marcus, you are literally the only person I've ever met that dislikes that show. It's funny. It's timeless. Accept it."

"I don't care if it supposedly belonged to their grandmother or whatever—there's no way they would've been able to afford an apartment that big in New York. And, believe it or not, black people do actually live in New York City."

I grimaced at that. I had no good retort. "I know. Two totally fair points." I unbuckled my seat belt and leaned over to kiss him. "Will you forgive me if I continue to adore that show?"

He laughed and turned to kiss me until I was entirely confident I was forgiven. "Of course. I know to try to convince you otherwise would be futile."

I laughed and pulled away. "Let's get inside and figure this thing out. We're close. I can tell."

"*K*nock. Knock." Near midnight—several hours into our think session in the study room—Sydney's voice called to us through the closed door.

Please let her have food. Please let her have food. Please let her have food.

The silent plea played over in my mind as I stood to open the door for her. Sydney was a ridiculously good cook, and I'd not eaten since that morning. I was starving.

I nearly kissed her when I pulled open the door to see her carrying a large tray of leftovers from dinner. "You're a saint, Sydney."

She winked at me as she stepped inside and Marcus hurried to clear a spot on the table for the tray. "No. I just have a sixth sense for growling stomachs. Plus, I've been curious about what you learned today. How did it go?"

Marcus filled her in as I dug right in on the best Chicken Parmesan I'd ever had in my life. Thoughtlessly, I interrupted him as I moaned in delight.

"If you weren't already married to Callum, I think I'd be down on one knee right now."

Marcus snorted and reached for his plate as Sydney laughed.

"I'm so glad you like it—now what was it you were saying, Marcus?"

I bent to continue enjoying my food as Marcus finished relaying everything we'd learned from the professor.

Once he was finished, Sydney began to drum her fingers on the table in thought. "Hmm...so I suppose that's what you guys are doing tonight? Trying to figure out the connection between all of the women who are to follow Kate and Laurel?"

I nodded with a mouthful of chicken.

"Well, count me in. I want to help." She quickly stepped away from the table before turning back to the door. "But first, while you two finish your food, I'm going to go tell Callum that I won't be to bed until late. Let's regroup in fifteen."

With Marcus' mouth now as full as mine, we waved her on to go and see to her husband.

"We've been working on this for hours. It won't surprise me one bit if Sydney comes in here and has it figured out in five minutes."

I laughed as I finally forced myself to shove the plate away from me. If I didn't stop soon, I would burst.

"Well, it's very possible that we've been so close to it for so long that we can't see what's right in front of us. Plus, Sydney is wicked sharp. Either way, I'm open to any help we can get."

He nodded in agreement. "Oh, me too."

The sudden sound of footsteps running down the hallway caused both of us to glance toward the door. I was certain it would be Olivia. Sydney hadn't possibly had time to find Callum yet.

To both of our surprise, it was Sydney who threw open the door.

"I've got it!"

Marcus stood and looked at her confused. "Got what?"

She threw up her hands in excitement. "How they're all connected. It's Morna, of course! The women aren't following you and Laurel and Kate. They came before you. They're already all there."

"Huh?" It was literally the only thing I could think of to say. I didn't know enough about this mysterious witch to follow Sydney's train of thought.

"Morna can't use her magic to help you all defeat Machara, but I think she's already helped the women get where they needed to be to do so. It's the others—the ones who already live in the past: Bri, Blaire, Mitsy, Grace, Kathleen, Jane, Laurel, Kate, and you—you are the nine!"

Marcus looked like he was about to fall over. "You're right. You have to be right, but what about you and Gillian? Morna played a hand in your lives, as well."

Sydney nodded as if she already had that all worked out. I was totally lost, but excitement built all the same. I could see that they were on to something. They could explain it all to me later.

"Yes, she did, but we live in the twenty-first century, not the seventeenth. All of the women you need to defeat Machara are already there. All we have to do is gather them up."

CHAPTER 34

Morna's Home - September – The Night of Ross' Visit

Morna remained near the fire long after the strange man left. Her heart was heavy, her mind unsure. Had she been wrong to send him away without giving him what he wanted?

No. Despite the man's grief, it wasn't magic she could do without first speaking to his wife. Deep inside, she knew the wisdom of her actions, but God, how she'd wanted to help him.

"Who was it, lass?"

She turned at the sound of her husband's voice as she motioned for Jerry to come and join her on the couch. She needed him near her, needed to lay her head down on his shoulder for the comfort his touch always provided her.

"I doona believe I ever got his real name, but I am certain I shall see him again."

She sighed as Jerry lowered himself next to her. His cheeks were rosy from the heat of his bath, his smile relaxed as he pulled her in close.

"Are ye all right, love? Ye look as if this man troubled ye."

Morna nodded as she allowed her head to relax on her husband's shoulder. She supposed now it made perfect sense why she'd woken in a panic two days earlier—desperate to get home—in the middle of their Australian vacation. She was needed. She'd felt it so acutely, they'd packed up right away. Now she knew why.

"Aye, I suppose I am, though I shall play only a small part in this story."

"Is this why we had to come back so quickly?"

"Aye, and I think 'tis time I let all those we love know we are home. I've a feeling they've been waiting for us for some time."

The call had come in the middle of the night, but that didn't stop Sydney from coming to our room straight away to tell us—Morna and Jerry were finally home.

It didn't take long for all of us to see that Sydney had to be right about the other women. As a result, she'd sent her husband, Callum, along with Gillian's husband, Orick, back to the seventeenth century to send word to all the women Morna had sent back to ask for their help.

It was a relief to know that one giant mystery was now solved, but we were still unable to return home.

Ross still had to be found, not only for my sake, but for the unanswered questions that The Eight had surrounding his powers. If there was any possibility that he could be the one to help save Freya, we had to find him.

It was abundantly clear that he had no intention of being found.

And so, while Callum and Orick went traveling throughout Scotland, we were in a state of purgatory, waiting for the famous Morna to return home.

Five hours after Sydney woke us with the news, we were in the car headed to Morna's home. By the time we arrived, I was sick with nerves. From everything that I'd heard about her, I knew Morna was an incredibly powerful witch. If she couldn't point us in the right direction for the spell that would save Freya, if she couldn't help us find Ross, then I doubted anyone would be able to.

The old woman and a man I assumed was her husband were standing in the doorway by the time Marcus and I stepped out of the car.

"Marcus, lad," Morna called after him. "Please tell me ye've forgiven me by now. I know I dinna send ye back in the gentlest way."

I glanced over at Marcus to see him smiling, though I knew he was nervous about what we might learn from her, too.

"I've forgiven you. Though I'd prefer it if you never use any of your magic on me again."

"Agreed."

She pulled him into a giant hug as the old man next to her stepped around them to meet me.

"My name is Jerry, lass."

I took his hand as I introduced myself. "I'm Silva. Thank you for letting us come over."

He hurried to dismiss my gratitude as he kept ahold of my hand and led me inside. "Nonsense, lass. 'Tis always a pleasure when we have company."

"Aye, lass. I've seen ye in my mind for some time now, though I know ye know nothing of me."

I couldn't begin to imagine what she meant by that, but I chose to ignore it as I allowed myself to be pulled into her welcoming embrace.

"I'll not bore either of ye with chit chat. Sydney made it clear that ye've been waiting on us to return home. Ye have questions for me, and I have much to tell ye. Let's not put it off another moment, aye?"

Pleased that she seemed intent to get right down to business, I reached behind for Marcus' hand as we followed the elderly couple inside.

Marcus bent down to whisper in my ear. "Morna is a bit of a matchmaker. I suppose she's had you picked out for me for awhile now."

I made a mental note to inquire about that and much more at a later time as we stepped into the cozy living room and took our seats.

Marcus jumped right in with his questions. "Morna, who are the nine women capable of defeating Machara? I know you like to take your time meddling and moving people around to wherever and whenever you think they need to be, but there's someone on The Isle that we all care about very much. We are running out of time to save her."

Morna gave Marcus a gentle smile. At the same time, I reached out to gently squeeze his knee. He might have forgiven Morna, but I still didn't get the feeling that he was overly fond of her.

"My timing has nothing to do with it, lad. I made a promise to a friend long ago to help defeat her in whatever way I could without unintentionally aiding Machara through the use of magic. My part in all of this is nearly complete."

He continued to prod her. "So the nine are already there? It's the women you've already sent back?"

She nodded. "Yes, but ye are wrong about one thing, Marcus. The legend says that magical beings such as ye and I canna defeat Machara, that her demise must come at the hands of mortal women. It doesna say anywhere that these mortal women canna use magic to defeat her."

"What?"

Marcus and I both asked the question in unison. How could mortal women—women without magical powers—use magic to defeat Machara?

"Think on it. Deep down ye already know. What is the one thing that would truly set each and every one of The Eight free?"

I knew right away as I looked at Marcus and thought back on what he'd told me just before we traveled forward through time.

They would have to give it up.

The Eight would have to sacrifice their magic and become entirely mortal once again.

It only took a second for Marcus to catch up with me, and as was no surprise, he didn't flinch in response. There was nothing he wouldn't do to see this all finally finished.

"Great. What do we have to do?"

Morna stood and moved to a shelf next to her fireplace. She latched onto an old book, took a quick look at it, and extended it in Marcus' direction.

"'Tis a simple spell. One ye can all do together once ye return home. It shall hurt like hell, but ye will all survive it, though I'm certain there are some among ye that will struggle with the loss of such power."

A thought occurred to me as I watched Marcus look down at the open spell. The Eight hadn't truly been eight since I'd known them. For over a year, Paton had been locked away in the land of the Fae. He wouldn't be free for almost another two years.

I spoke up, my voice shaking from what I knew had to be true.

"We will have to have the magic of eight men, yes?"

Morna nodded, and I could see in her gaze that our thoughts were on the same path.

"Aye."

"But there are only seven of them."

She didn't break eye contact with me as she spoke. "There is another with magic who should have been with them all along. I believe I met him last night."

I could scarcely breathe as I realized that I was sitting in a space Ross had so recently occupied. It made the fact that I knew he was alive seem so much more real, and I realized that I wasn't nearly as prepared to handle all of this as I thought.

"Ross?"

She gave me a sad smile. "Is that his real name, then? Aye, lass. Ross."

CHAPTER 35

*S*he thought she was his. Marcus knew that she loved him. He knew that she wanted to give him every piece of her heart, but she wasn't there yet, no matter how much he wanted her to be.

He could see it in the way she winced when Morna mentioned meeting another with magic only the night before, and the way she'd said his name had been like a dagger through his heart.

They knew what they needed to do to save Freya. He would drag that bastard Ross back to the seventeenth century kicking and screaming if he had to, but all of that was talk for another day. The moment Ross' name was mentioned, the evening became Silva's. She needed to hear anything that Morna could tell her. She needed answers that he couldn't give her. So as he braced for words he knew would hurt him, words he knew would threaten all that they'd built together over the past year, he sat back and allowed himself to blend in with the furniture.

He would listen with his whole heart. He would gauge Silva's every expression, and he would hope with all he had that by the time this night was over, he would have some clarity about the best way to help the woman he so desperately loved.

"Ross was here, Morna? Do you know him? Why would he come to you?"

He didn't miss the way Morna cast a cautious glance at him, but he refused to meet her gaze. This wasn't about him. It didn't matter how uncomfortable this might make him. She needed to hear it—it was about her—and that was enough to make him capable of handling anything.

"No, I doona know him, lass. Last night was the first time I ever laid eyes on him. And although he used a different name, I know 'twas Ross. I can see the anger ye have for him in yer eyes, Silva. I doona blame ye, but mayhap ye wish to know some of what ye doona, aye?"

Marcus couldn't bring himself to look at her. He didn't want to see the hurt in her eyes, and he didn't want her to take notice of him and refrain from speaking freely.

He only knew she nodded when Morna began to speak again.

"Yer husband was wrong to do what he did. He should have trusted ye. He should have told ye what he saw that day he decided to fake his own death. He should have allowed ye to make the choice on yer own. I canna say what made him do as he did, but I can tell ye this: it broke his heart to leave ye, and there hasna been a day since he parted from ye that he hasna hated himself for it."

Marcus had to bite down on his own lip to keep himself from gathering her up in his arms when she broke down into sobs.

*I*t never occurred to me that Ross hadn't wanted to leave me. The moment I learned he was alive, I felt rejected, unwanted, and used. How could you love someone the way I thought he'd loved me and then leave? What could have possibly torn him away?

I struggled to speak between sobs as confusion overtook every other thought in my mind. "Then why did he leave me? It doesn't make any sense."

She sighed, and I could see she was reluctant to answer me. "I will tell ye as I told him. There is unfinished business between ye. He should be the one to answer any questions ye have."

"But why was he here? Why did he come to see you?"

I was having difficulty breathing. My chest hurt, my head felt light. I bent down to put my head in between my legs.

"Lass, did he not tell ye when ye married him how it works with those that hold magic?"

I would have laughed if I'd had the lung capacity to do so.

I lifted my head just long enough to answer her.

"Surely, you can see there are many things he didn't tell me."

She sighed again. I knew my reaction was causing her distress. I couldn't help it.

"Ye are bound to him, lass. Yer heart is tied to his. He can feel ye when ye are near to him. Having ye in this time was torturing him. He came so that I would break that bond."

No wonder I felt as if I could never truly move on from him. Part of my heart literally no longer belonged to me.

"And you wouldn't do it? Why?"

I felt her hands suddenly on my knees, and I looked up to see her crouched down in front of me. I knew she was using magic, for as her hands gently patted my legs, my breathing began to calm.

"I couldna do so, lass, not without ye agreeing to the break, as well. Ye need to go to him. If ye wish for me to break the bond between ye after ye have spoken with him, I shall do so. For now though, ye need some rest."

I was growing increasingly sleepy. I didn't want to sleep. I was far too confused and hurt for it, but the edges of my vision were beginning to blur.

I heard Morna mumble some sort of direction to Marcus, and my last conscious memory was that of his arms coming around me as he lifted me into his arms.

"*W*hat is on yer mind, lad?"

Hours had passed since he'd carried Silva upstairs and placed her in the bed where they would both spend the night. For hours, Morna had allowed him to sit silently while he thought.

"I don't want to lose her, Morna. I'm not sure what my life will look like if I do."

Pulling his gaze away from the fire, he accepted her hand as she offered it to him.

"What makes ye think ye will lose her, lad?"

The sound of her sobs still rang through his mind. The pain in her eyes was all he could see. The way tears ran down her cheeks as she finally succumbed to Morna's sleep spell would stay with him forever.

"You saw her, Morna. She loves him still. It was different for her when she believed he'd wanted to leave her. But if he still wants her, what is there to keep her from going back to him?"

She squeezed his hand, and he had to swallow the lump that rose in his throat as his own tears threatened to spill.

"Ye. Ye are what will keep her from going back to him. Ye need to have faith in what she feels for ye. Ye know in yer heart that 'tis true."

"Yes, but that doesn't mean she doesn't also love him."

Morna brought his hand to her mouth and kissed it with such tenderness that he could no longer hold back his tears.

"But, dear boy, ye are forgetting one thing. You will give her a choice where he gave her none. That alone will mean more to her than ye can possibly know."

Morna was right. The choice had to be hers.

He knew exactly what he needed to do.

CHAPTER 36

*J*ust as the sun was beginning to rise, I woke to the sudden warmth of Marcus' body as he crawled into bed with me. I turned toward him, eager for the safety and comfort of his arms. My head on his chest was my favorite place in the world, and I needed it now more than I'd ever needed it in my life.

Sleep—no matter how much I wanted to fight it—had kept me from coming completely undone.

"What time is it?" I whispered to him as he pulled me against him.

"It's early. It's okay if you need to sleep a little longer. I just wanted to hold you for a while."

I smiled as I snuggled into him, but I could feel how tight his muscles were beside me. As my eyes adjusted to the dim light, I looked up at him and noticed that the corner of his eye was damp.

"I'm awake." I pushed myself up off his chest to look down at him. "Marcus, what's wrong?"

He rose up enough to pull me down for a kiss. "Nothing is wrong. But Morna cast a spell to locate Ross. He's living in Edinburgh. I've arranged for Jerry to drive you as soon as you are ready to go this morning. After breakfast, I'm taking Sydney's car, and I'm driving back to Cagair."

"What?" Everything about what he'd just said felt wrong. I couldn't see Ross without him. I wasn't strong enough.

He must have read my mind. "You have to do this on your own, Silva. You'll regret it if you don't. You need time with him to decide what you really want, to get the answers that you deserved long ago. I won't deny you that. I love you too much.

"And Silva..." He paused as he reached to gather up both my hands. "I'll understand if you decide to go back to him. He was your first love. I know the power of that. You don't owe me anything."

I threw my arms around him as I rushed to protest. "I owe you everything, Marcus."

He stroked my hair and I felt his chest vibrate as he let out a rough sob. "No, Silva. You have that backwards, love. It's you who gave me something I thought I would never have once I accepted my life in the seventeenth century. If I have to say goodbye to you now, it was worth it."

I pulled back and gripped his face so he would look at me. "You're not saying goodbye to me. I'll go and speak to him. I'll see things settled between us. Then I'm bringing Ross back to Cagair so we can all return to The Isle and finish Machara once and for all. But I'm returning to you, Marcus. You are the man I love. You're the one I see in my future."

I'd never seen such pain in his eyes before as he gently pushed me away from him and stood up. "You can't know that yet. Please don't make me promises now that might break my heart later. I love you, Silva, but right now your heart belongs to two men. Whether you realize it or not, you're still not sure which one of us you love more."

I was shaking as I watched him leave me alone in the barely lit bedroom. I wasn't cold, but part of me knew he was right, and nothing terrified me more.

CHAPTER 37

Edinburgh, Scotland

"Breathe, lass. Ye need to breathe."

I smiled as Jerry reached over the middle console of his car so that he could gently grab my hand.

It was only then I realized that I actually was holding my breath, and I drew in a long, shaky one at Jerry's command.

"Are ye frightened of him, lass? If ye need me to stay with ye, I will. At the verra least, I can stay for a little while until ye are comfortable."

I gave his hand a little squeeze. "No, I'm not frightened of him. I'm frightened of myself. Ross has always had a way of overwhelming me. I'm afraid of losing myself to him once again."

According to Jerry's navigation system, we were only a few blocks away. With each turn, my anxiety grew.

He surprised me by slowly pulling over to the side of the road before placing the car in park and turning toward me.

He reached over and grabbed my free hand so that he held onto both of them tightly.

"Do ye mind if an old man gives ye a piece of advice?"

I smiled and shook my head. "Go right ahead."

He winked at me before continuing. "No man can overwhelm ye. Ye are not the same lass ye were a year ago. I know ye and I are strangers, lass. I doona know ye, but I know this—ye have been to hell and back this past year, and ye survived it. Ye led a clan on yer own when ye werena even born in this century. And because of ye and Marcus, that wee bitch of a faerie will be sent to her death before year's end. Ye are the one with power, lass. Not the coward that abandoned ye because he dinna think ye could handle the truth.

"If ye walk into his home with anything other than yer head held high and yer eyes clear of tears, ye will regret it every day of yer life. This is yer moment to show him the woman he gave up. This is the time to show him the woman ye have become, not because of him, but in spite of him. Do ye hear me, lass?"

Tears streaming down my face, I pulled my hands away from him and threw my arms around his neck.

"You're incredible, Jerry. There is nothing I needed to hear more."

He smiled and turned back toward the wheel. "Good. Now, let's go pay the bastard a visit."

---

*H*e was losing his mind, he was sure of it. He could feel her heart beating closer and closer to him, could feel the anxious catch of her breath.

Was she really close to him, or was his misery making him mad?

Nothing would dull the pain in his chest. Booze, sleep, women —it was always there, punishing him, reminding him of what a foolish coward he was.

A knock on his door caused him to sit upright in his bed.

It was her.

He knew it without looking.

How could he let her see him like this?

How could he not?

She would hate him, he was sure of it. The confidence he'd shown Morna about whom Silva would choose was a façade—a little piece of hope that helped keep him sane.

What did it matter anyway?

She couldn't possibly hate him more than he already hated himself.

His breath was ragged as he pulled open the door.

And there she was.

Perfect.

More beautiful than she'd ever been.

He could mutter only one word.

"Silva."

CHAPTER 38

*J*erry might've been right about me not being the same woman I was when Ross left me, but Ross certainly wasn't the same man.

I wasn't sure what I expected, but it wasn't the broken man standing in front of me.

I barely recognized him. In truth, if I'd passed him on the street, I wasn't sure that I would have.

He said my name with such agony in his voice that I nearly dropped to my knees.

I hoped he couldn't see my hands shaking as I stood there. I hoped Jerry couldn't see it either as I turned back over my shoulder to solemnly wave him on.

I waited until Jerry turned the corner at the end of the street before facing Ross once more.

He repeated my name, but this time he didn't have the strength to remain standing. As he dropped to his knees and began to cry, I pulled him to me instinctively, wrapping my arms around his head as I held him against my stomach.

Any anger I felt toward this man was gone in an instant. He

looked as if every bit of grief I'd felt over the entire year had suddenly hit him at once.

His tears soaked my shirt as I held him, stroking his hair. I held my breath to keep from sobbing along with him. Only when I noticed a mother pushing her stroller down the street, staring at us with concern did I push him away long enough to speak.

"Let's go inside, Ross."

He yanked back as if my words woke him from a stupor. Shaking his head, he stood and held the door open for me as I stepped inside the small, sparse, dingy apartment.

Without a word, I followed him over to the worn and lumpy couch and lowered myself down next to him.

"Silva, I…I'm so sorry, lass." His voice broke again. I deserved an apology from him, but with each minute that I spent in his presence, I was beginning to wonder if perhaps I'd had more power over him all along than I realized.

Yes, he overwhelmed me. Yes, I'd found his love to be all-consuming, but perhaps, it had been no different for him.

It helped me somehow. It evened the playing field in a way that helped me look at him with the empathy I knew I would need to survive this night.

This wasn't a man justifying his wretched actions. This was a man broken by guilt and remorse. This man had missed me just as much as I'd missed him.

"I know, Ross, but you have to tell me why. You have to tell me why you did it. I don't understand."

He took a deep, unsteady breath and closed his eyes as if to gain his composure. Then he began to speak. "'Tis a long story, lass."

"I've got all the time you need. I've been waiting a very long time to hear it."

He sighed and reached for my hands. It wasn't until he began to stroke them as he'd done a million times before that I realized perhaps I shouldn't have allowed him to touch me so easily. It was just automatic with Ross. There was too much history, too many habits that wouldn't die easily.

"When I was young, I made a cowardly and selfish decision to run from a fate that should've been mine."

I interrupted to confirm what Marcus and I already suspected.

"You were supposed to be one of The Eight?"

He nodded. "Aye, but ye know me, Silva. I've too solitary a nature, too wild of a streak inside me to be beholden to a destiny outside of that which I make for myself. I couldna do it, so I fled to this time, and by doing so, I sent a man who shoulda been laird to be a servant to one."

I thought of Raudrich. Ross' worry was for naught. For as long as I'd been at Castle Murray, Raudrich was more the leader of the keep than Nicol.

"If it will ease your guilt a little, Raudrich is servant to no one."

Ross shook his head before looking down at our combined hands.

"I should feel guilt for leaving, but I havena regretted it for a single day. Leaving allowed me to meet ye, and ye have been the joy of my life. If only I'd never taken ye there, perhaps I wouldna have had to hurt ye so."

I understood why we'd gone back. Even if he didn't feel guilty that his decision had changed Raudrich's life, he still cared for his friend. He'd wanted to be there to help when Raudrich's brother was killed. It was everything after that time that made no sense to me.

"What happened there, Ross? What made you believe you needed to leave me there?"

I listened as he spoke of the mountaintop and the well I'd seen on my visit to throw away my ring. As I listened, much of my anger returned.

"But Ross, if you saw me at The Isle, if you believed that it was my destiny to be there, why not just take me there yourself?"

He looked up from our hands and into my eyes as his gaze pleaded with me to understand. "Do ye truly believe that 'twas not exactly what I wished to do? The pool showed me more than just ye. It showed me the man ye are with now, lass. The other member of The Eight whom ye now love."

I swallowed uncomfortably. "You saw Marcus?"

His voice sounded strangled as he answered. "Aye. Never in my life have I wanted to kill a man more, but while I could choose to run from my destiny, how could I allow ye to do the same? I couldna do so. So I left ye, knowing that in time yer destiny would find ye. And so it seems, it has."

Stunned, I sat there silently as my mind sorted through the barrage of thoughts that fought for my attention.

"You should have given me a choice, Ross. If you saw that my future wasn't with you, you should have told me. It should've been up to me all along."

He gave me a gentle smile, and it was the first time I could see that part of the man I'd known still remained inside him.

"Silva, lass, yer heart was as much mine then as mine will be yers forever. Ye wouldna have believed me had I told ye. Even if I had, ye would've fought like hell against it. Ye would have fled with me back to this time. Ye would've damned them all. Without ye, Machara canna be killed. I may be a selfish arse of a man, and while I could send my best friend to a duty that should have never been his, I couldna send him to his death. And without ye, lass, they all die."

As much as I hated it, I knew Ross was right. I would have done anything to stay with him. At that time, death was the only way I would have ever let him go.

I looked at him, at the pain in his eyes, and all I could feel for him was love. He saw himself as selfish, but that was the very last thing he was.

By grieving him, my heart had been allowed to heal. By

believing that he was gone, I'd been given the opportunity to love again. What had this year been like for him? What would it have been like for me had our roles been reversed?

Would I have been able to let him go even if I knew he was meant for someone else when everything in me still loved him as much as it ever had?

I knew the answer was no.

I pulled him close to me as I kissed his cheek before moving my hands to either side of his face as I spoke to him.

He was still the man I'd known. He was still the kind, loving, adventurous man I'd fallen for, but circumstances beyond him had broken him, and all he'd done was respond in the best way he knew how.

"Ross, you have to forgive yourself. You are not a selfish man. What you did as a boy wasn't selfish. It was sensible. All you knew was that you didn't want to be bound to anyone else. You had no way of knowing what that would mean for Raudrich. And what you've done now..." I paused as my own tears spilled over. Once again, I was overwhelmed by him but for a very different reason. "It is the bravest, most selfless thing I've ever seen anyone do."

He surprised me by laughing. "Doona fool yerself, lass. If I truly believed that enough of yer heart still belonged to me for ye to be happy, I would take ye right here on this couch and never let ye go again. I am only able to do this because I know I have lost."

I couldn't argue with him. I held as much love in my heart for Ross as I did anyone on earth, but I was no longer in love with him, and he knew it. We had to break the bond between us, but first I needed to know if he could live in pain for a while longer to save yet another life.

"Ross?"

He pulled his face away from my hands and gathered them in his lap once again. "Aye?"

"I know you've already given up so much for me, but there's

something else—something that I have no right to ask of you—that I need you to do."

He bent to kiss my hand, and my heart squeezed with love for him. "Canna ye see, lass? There is nothing I wouldna do for ye—even tear out my own heart."

CHAPTER 39

Cagair Castle

It was three-thirty in the morning when I pulled Ross' car into the driveway of Cagair Castle. I'd called ahead so Sydney would have a room ready for Ross, but I'd asked her to say nothing to Marcus.

I knew he wasn't expecting me back so soon, and even though I hated it, I knew part of him worried that he wouldn't ever have me back in the way he wanted. I couldn't wait to tell him how wrong he was.

Ross and I spent the day making peace with our past, talking and reminiscing. Finally, after everything had been said that needed to be, we made a plan for how we would try to defeat Machara, and ultimately save Freya.

It wasn't foolproof. There was so much that could go wrong.

Ross might have avoided being one of The Eight for most of his life, but in the end, his destiny would be as tied to The Isle as mine was.

"Should I be worried that this man will try to harm me?"

I gave Ross a disappointed look as I turned off the engine and quietly stepped out of the car. "You're going to have to be around him. Call him Marcus. I'm afraid you should be much more worried about Olivia's reaction to you. She's promised to bloody your nose."

He winced, and I knew he was sufficiently frightened. He knew Olivia—he knew that she rarely made false threats.

I heard the soft sound of rocks crunching beneath someone's feet and turned to see Sydney approaching, her hand extended toward Ross. "You must be Ross. I have a room ready for you." She glanced over at me. "Silva, I'll see him taken care of. We'll see you in the morning."

I suspected she'd seen how distressed Marcus had been after returning to the castle without me. Giving her a quick nod of appreciation, I hurried up to our bedroom to reassure the man I loved.

*arcus slept soundly. I was naked and tucked into the nook of his arm, gently trailing kisses along his jaw before he woke and realized that I was there. Instinctively, he turned into me and began to kiss me. It took him a moment to remember that I shouldn't be there, but when he did realize, he jerked away with such intensity that he nearly jumped off the bed.

"Silva? You…you're…did you not find him?"

I shook my head. "No, we found him. He's here, Marcus. He's going back with us, and we have a plan."

He held up a hand to stop me. "Wait a minute. So, you've already visited with Ross? And you're okay? And you're in my bed?"

I reached for him and as he leaned against the headboard, I climbed on top of him, straddling his lap as I smiled at him. "Yes.

I'm not ever leaving your bed again. I told you it was you, Marcus. It's been you for a long time now."

That was all he needed to hear tonight. I could tell him our plan in the morning. For now, I just needed to feel him. I needed to love him. I needed to kiss away any remaining doubt inside his mind.

"Take me, Marcus. Make me yours."

His mouth was on mine in an instant, his hardness pressing against me, urging me to rise up enough to take him inside.

I didn't stop showing him how much he meant to me until daylight streamed in through the shades and the bustling noises of the castle could be heard outside our door.

S ydney brought us breakfast in bed. I was beginning to think that the overly energetic woman never slept. As we munched on our quiche and muffins, I explained to Marcus what we'd worked out.

"Ross is willing to sacrifice his magic along with the rest of you, but none of you can give it up until Freya is restored to life. He thinks we have to convince Machara to break her bond with Freya before you all do anything."

I could see the skepticism on his face.

"She will never do it."

Ross and I had debated on this for hours. After lots of conversation, I truly believed it might work.

"Machara doesn't know about Ross or his magic, and she isn't going to know until it's too late for her. Ross—as Raudrich already knows—has the ability to shield his magic from others with such powers. As far as Machara knows, there's only the magic of seven keeping her caged. Nicol has been away from the castle for months. If we can convince her that you are desperate to return to your old life, that you're tired of serving a laird who refuses to rule, she might make you a bargain."

He interrupted me, as I expected. "What sort of bargain?"

"You're going to tell her that you want to return to your old life, but that you've grown too fond of Freya to let her die. You've been there less time than the others. She doesn't really know you, and she's vulnerable right now. If you can convince her, it just might work. Tell her that if she will break her bond to Freya, you will use your magic to see her restored to life and then you will give it up and become mortal once again."

Marcus looked at me like it was the stupidest plan he'd ever heard. "She will suspect that I'm lying to her."

"Which is why you will make her a blood oath that you are telling the truth." When he stared wordlessly at me like I'd sprouted another head, I continued, "Everything will have to move rather quickly. The other men will have to be in place, and Ross will have to be ready with the spell for Freya, but it's the best chance we have."

"And what happens once we sacrifice our magic? Where does it go? Machara will be free in an instant. How will the rest of you defeat her?"

"It will transfer to us women, but only for a short amount of time. Just long enough for each of us to say our part of the spell to Machara. Laurel and Kate will be doing double duty. They've already weakened her significantly, but they will own part of the spell as well."

He continued to question me. "But it says that each woman must best her. How will you do that if you cast the spell all at once?"

"We won't. I'll go first, and my part of the spell—if all goes according to plan—will stun her within her cage long enough for the rest to go to her one-by-one before she has time to escape. She will give each woman hell, I'm sure of it, but none of us can know exactly how. It will take all of our strength, individually, to best her. If we can each overcome whatever she throws at us and cast our part of the spell, she will die, and finally, all of this will be over."

Marcus closed his eyes, shook his head, and sighed. "None of this sounds like very good odds."

I nodded and reached out to grab his hand. "We've known that all along, Marcus. In the end, it was always going to be dicey."

CHAPTER 40

*S*hortly after Marcus and I finished breakfast, I slipped away to wake Olivia. I wanted to find her before she found Ross. Now that I knew the truth, now that I'd seen precisely how much he was still hurting, I wasn't about to let her attack him —no matter how well-meaning her intentions were.

She was still fast asleep when I entered her bedroom, the television remote still tightly gripped in her hand. It was slightly disturbing how quickly she'd taken on so many terrible habits of twenty-first century life. It was time for us to get Olivia home.

"Liv," I gave her arm a gentle shake as her eyelids reluctantly fluttered open. "I'm back."

She smiled and raised up in the bed, her hair sticking up in ten different directions.

"I told Marcus there was no reason for him to worry. I doona think it did much good though. So…" She paused and scooted over to pat the bed so I would sit down. "Did ye tell the bastard just where he could go, then?"

I scrunched up my nose nervously at her. "No, but we had a nice, long talk. Things are okay now."

Her eyes bulged and she lifted her eyebrows in shock. "You had a nice long talk? Are ye out of yer mind, Silva? Doona ye remember what he did to ye? What he...what he did to all of us?" Her voice broke, and in that instant I realized something that I'd been too self-absorbed until now to realize—I wasn't the only one who'd grieved him.

"Oh, Liv." I pulled her into my arms as she cried. "I've been a pretty terrible stepsister. You loved him too."

She nodded in my arms. "Aye. O'course I did, but I'm so angry with him."

I kissed the top of her head. "Please, don't be. If I promise you that everything he did was for a good reason and that it pained him more than either of us will ever understand, will you forgive him? He's here, Liv. He's going back with us to help defeat Machara. I know he would love to see you."

She sniffled, and I could feel some of the tension from her shoulders relax. "I doona suppose I'm allowed to hit him if ye've forgiven him, aye?"

I shrugged. I knew better than to give her an outright order. "If it would really make you feel better, then go for it."

She laughed and pushed away from me as she crawled from the bed. "I truly would like to see him."

"Get dressed. I'll walk you over to his room. I won't be surprised if he's still sleeping. Yesterday was difficult for him."

I watched Olivia as she started to walk toward the wardrobe on the opposite wall. She suddenly stopped and backtracked over to the window that looked out over the front lawn of the castle. Her eyes widened.

"What is it?"

"'Tis Ross. He...he's sitting on the steps outside with Marcus."

*T*he conversation was inevitable. He couldn't ride side-by-side with the man for days without having had a conversation with him away from Silva. Ross was a stranger to him, but they had much in common. And regardless of how he felt about it, The Eight needed him. Freya needed him.

They needed to be on the same page.

He left quickly after Silva went to wake Olivia, making his way down to the castle's kitchen to inquire after Ross' whereabouts from Sydney.

The endlessly busy woman greeted him the moment he stepped inside. "How was breakfast?"

"Amazing, as always. Have you seen Ross?"

She looked at him carefully for a moment, and he hurried to reassure her.

"I just want to talk to him."

She nodded, and pointed in the direction of the front of the castle. "Said he needed some air and was going for a walk. You'll find him somewhere outside."

He didn't have to look far. Ross was seated on the first step outside of the castle, almost as if he was waiting for him.

The man didn't turn toward him, but the moment Marcus sat down beside him, he spoke. "Do ye love her as much as she loves ye?"

It made it difficult for him to dislike the man when he could hear the agony in his voice. "I love her more than she loves me. I always will."

For the first time, Ross turned toward him. "Then, mayhap ye are worthy of her. I wouldna be here now if I dinna have to be. I will help see this ended for her sake and for the sake of everyone on The Isle. Then I will go, and Silva will never see me again. The moment I surrender my powers with the rest of ye, my bond to Silva will be broken. I willna stand in yer way."

Knowing that an understanding had been struck, he extended the man his hand just as Sydney stepped outside to join them.

"Callum just arrived. Everyone is headed to Castle Murray. It's time for all of you to return home."

CHAPTER 41

he Isle of Eight Lairds - 1653

icol was still gone when we arrived at the castle, which played to the strength of our plan. Everyone knew it was a risk. If Marcus couldn't convince Machara to strike a bargain with him, if Ross' spell didn't work, then Freya's life would most likely come to its final end—all without Nicol ever having a chance to say goodbye.

With the castle bursting at the seams with guests, we held talks for days, going over every detail until everyone involved was on board.

The only one that was left in the dark was Freya—though we all hated it. While Freya had reassured us all many times before that Machara couldn't hear her thoughts or conversations, we couldn't risk Machara picking up on Freya's change of mood. We all just had to hope that it would all work out for the best and we could ask both Freya and Nicol for forgiveness later.

Sex hadn't been enough to relax Marcus. As I lay there, fully sated and wrapped up in his arms, I could hear the rapid intake and exhale of his breath, and I knew just how stressed and frightened he was.

"It's going to be okay, Marcus."

He sighed and rolled toward me so that we faced each other in the bed. "We can't know that, Silva. If this all goes south..." He hesitated. "She could kill all of us. What if my part in this dooms us all? What if I'm toying with too much magic?"

"You tricking Machara into a bargain isn't going to defeat her. You're using magic to save Freya. You're not breaking the rules. And Machara isn't going to kill us. I know she won't. This ends in our favor, Marcus. And when all of this is done, do you know what I want to do?"

"What?"

I leaned forward to kiss him before moving to whisper in his ear, "I want to marry you."

He yanked back and looked at me with shock. "That is not how I wanted it to be for you. I'm supposed to be the one to do that, Silva."

I waved a dismissive hand. I didn't need that from him. I just needed him to be mine, and I needed him to believe that he could trick Machara into a bargain.

"Hogwash. This is exactly how I wanted it to be. You still haven't given me an answer though..."

He crushed his mouth to mine, and as he crawled on top of me he whispered the word *yes* over and over as he trailed kisses down my body.

By the time we finally left our bedroom that morning, Marcus was ready.

It was time to save Freya.

It was time for that bitch to die.

"Why would ye betray yer brothers in such a way? Have they ever wronged ye?"

Marcus steeled himself against Machara's icy gaze. He wasn't worried for himself, but he wouldn't ever be able to forgive himself if he failed Freya. Words were of the utmost importance when it came to conversations with Machara. He would have to say what was as close to the truth as possible.

"I wasn't born in this time, Machara. I miss my old life, my old friends. I miss making decisions for myself without taking others into account. And yes, they wronged me the day they bound me to them against my will."

Machara stepped nearer to the bars that bound her, looking stronger than she'd looked in months. Marcus could see how desperate they'd made her by leaving her in isolation for so long. It would make her vulnerable to his proposal.

"Ye saw what Calder's betrayal did to them, yet what ye propose would end them. Years of service and ye would see me freed in an instant? Their sacrifice would be for naught. Surely ye are not as evil as that."

He kept his gaze steady, refusing to break eye contact with her as he answered, "I'm not evil. I just want to go home."

"And ye care more for Freya's soul than ye do for anyone else in the castle?"

"I do. Nicol has left us, Machara. I have given up my life for a man that isn't worthy of it. He is free to go wherever he pleases while I must remain here to keep you locked away—you who have never done anything to me. I was never part of this, Machara. I just want it all to end."

She crossed her arms as she drummed her long fingernails against her arm. "And ye will end it? Ye will sacrifice yer magic if I will free Freya from her bond to me, allowing ye to restore her to her body, even though ye know Paton is locked away with my father?"

He nodded.

"How do ye even know such magic? Yer powers havena been with ye long enough."

"I have been searching for a way to save Freya for over a year now. I wouldn't have come to you now unless I was certain I'd mastered the spell required to restore her once you break your bond to her."

For a moment, Machara said nothing, and Marcus knew she was beginning to believe.

"Ye must know that I canna agree to this based on yer word."

He pulled the small dagger from his kilt, and carefully cut open the palm of his hand. "Yes. I know. I shall make you a blood oath. Once Freya is no longer bound to you and I have gone to her grave to cast the spell to restore her life, I will relinquish my magic."

"And then I shall be free. For with only six men, ye canna keep me."

He nodded. "Exactly. Have we reached a bargain?"

Machara slipped her arm through the bars in front of her, extending her palm in his direction as she awaited his blood.

"Begin the spell to free Freya. I won't offer you my blood until you do so."

As Machara began to speak the words aloud, the air around them began to heat.

Taking a breath for courage, he lifted his bleeding palm over hers and allowed his blood to drop onto her hand.

*W*e all stood ready around Freya's grave as we waited for something to happen.

The wait seemed to last forever, then in an instant, the leaves around her grave began to whirl and Ross began to shout the spell as he felt the bond between Machara and Freya break.

He screamed the spell aloud to the sky.
Everything fell silent, and we all turned toward Freya's casket.
She was gone.

CHAPTER 42

"*D*id it work?"

I screamed the question at Ross as we stared down at the empty casket. I didn't know what I'd expected, but it wasn't that she would just be gone.

He turned worried eyes on me. "I canna say for sure, lass, but right now, it doesna matter. We've only minutes before Machara realizes that another—nae Marcus—has cast the spell for Freya. We must all gather in the garden and surrender our powers now."

Together, we ran back to the garden where the rest of the women stood gathered. Marcus arrived just as we did, and I hurried to throw my arms around him. He was trembling all over.

"Are you okay?"

"Yes, but we have to hurry. Is everyone here?"

Henry called out to Marcus as we all gathered in the circle we'd practiced the night before.

"Aye. 'Tis time."

I reached up to kiss him before taking my place beside Bri, the first woman Morna ever sent back.

Despite my fear, as I looked down the row of women beside me,

I knew we would succeed. They were strong, smart, and we all knew our part of the spell by heart.

The men would cast Machara out of her cage and into the garden where they would hold her with their magic until the last moment it was surrendered.

At the exact moment the magic began to transfer, the men would flee the garden, for they knew they could play no part in this. It would all be up to us in the end.

Henry, the eldest of The Eight spoke.

"Are ye ready, lads? 'Tis time for us to give Machara a view outside her dungeon one last time before she dies."

It had taken no effort for us to convince the men that they would have to sacrifice their powers. They would all have to find a new way of living, but at least this time the choices about their futures would be theirs.

In unison, they chanted words none of us could understand. Slowly the garden took on the same sickly green hue as Machara's dungeon. When she appeared before us, there were no bars around her, but I could see from the way she stood that she couldn't move more than a few feet in any direction.

She looked at Marcus and reared back and laughed. "'Tis time, then? We shall finally see if my father's curse will hold true."

No one acknowledged her. We all just grasped hands as the men continued their spell, one by one saying the words that would break their bond to one another and rid them of their powers for good.

None of us knew exactly how it would happen, but Ross was certain I would know when it was time for me to cast my part of the spell, and I did.

The moment Henry dropped to the ground, releasing his grip on my hand and that of Ludo's, Machara began to smile, and the air around us began to crackle.

Turning toward her, I spoke the otherworldly language. As if it were a song, I allowed the words to blend together. One by one, the eight men dropped to their knees.

It took a moment for Machara to understand, but I saw when she tried to take her first free step that it stunned her when she could not.

The moment I finished and stepped back, Bri stepped forward. When she began to recite her words, both she and Machara disappeared, and we knew that Bri was facing whatever battle Machara had in store for her.

I glanced back at the remaining women. Fear was evident in each face, but determination was there, as well. We had all fought for too much before. We all had way too much at stake.

Olivia and Jimmie stood on the edge of the garden, watching in horror as the eight now mortal men struggled to stand. It took no time for them to react. Together, they helped lead the men from the garden. Giving up their magic had cost them strength I imagined it would take days for them to get back.

As quickly as she'd gone, Bri reappeared in the garden. Blaire wasted no time taking her stand, and in a flash, she was gone, as well.

We said nothing to one another as we waited, our only reassurance that each had succeeded was their reappearance in the garden.

When Kate—the last of us—disappeared, I was certain none of us dared to breathe. When she returned and nothing happened, dread and panic settled in my gut.

We'd missed something.

Machara wasn't dead.

I glanced over at the book near where Henry had fallen, and I knew.

We all had our own part, but it was something we would all have to finish together.

"We have to surrender the magic back. We weren't meant to hold it. It won't leave us on its own."

I ran for the book as we hurried to latch hands.

Once we stood together, I began to sound the words aloud, the rest of the women joining as they learned the rhythm of the words.

Our surroundings changed at once as we stood before Machara in a realm that had to be that of the fae.

Gone was the glow that always radiated from her. Gone was the anger in her eyes.

She no longer looked like the supernatural being she'd once been. She was beaten, and she knew it.

Together we returned the magic inside us to the land of the fae.

The residents of Castle Murray no longer had use of it.

Machara was finally dead, and The Isle of Eight Lairds was free.

CHAPTER 43

Two Weeks Later – October 1653

For weeks, things seemed to be at a standstill around the castle. Weak and weary, we all rested, but we all worried, as well. Freya was nowhere to be found. Her body was gone from its grave, and her spirit no longer appeared in the garden each night.

Nicol also remained missing.

Everything in his life had now changed, and Castle Murray's master was none the wiser.

To make matters worse, Ross and the former members of The Eight were too weak to go in search of him.

With Laurel and Kate by my side, we stood by the castle stables as we watched Bri, Blaire, Mitsy, Grace, Kathleen, and Jane, along with their husbands, ready themselves for their journey home.

We would always owe them a debt, but I suspected they all knew we would be there for them if the need ever arose.

"Silva?"

I turned toward Laurel's voice beside me.

"Yes."

"I've been thinking these past few days. I know that Ross will be ready to leave here as soon as he's strong enough. Do you know where he will go?"

I knew he would be apt to return to the twenty-first century. He would've been happy for us to have spent our lives there if everything hadn't gone so awry. Although I doubted either Scotland or New York City would hold much appeal for him anymore.

"I expect he will be eager to start over somewhere new."

Laurel nodded knowingly. "I kind of expected that. I'd like to offer him something, if you think he would take it."

"What's that?"

"My apartment in Boston and my bank savings until he figures out what he wants to do to support himself. I can have Sydney set everything up if you think he'd be interested."

It gave me more relief than Laurel would ever understand for me to know that Ross would at least have some place to go once he left here. He deserved happiness no matter the mistakes that he'd made. I hoped one day he would find it.

"I think he'd be more than interested."

She smiled and stepped away from me so we could go and bid everyone goodbye.

"Great. I'll talk to him about it before dinner tonight."

---

*E*veryone was finishing up dinner when the dining hall doors burst open and Nicol strolled inside, smiling widely, as if there was nothing strange at all about his sudden reappearance at the castle.

Raudrich—who'd grown increasingly angry with their master

each day he'd stayed away—burst out of his seat with more energy than he'd shown in days.

"Where the hell have ye been? Ye willna believe what has happened since ye've been away!"

Nicol laughed and walked over to his place at the end of the table as he waved Raudrich back down to his seat.

"I know what has happened. We are all finally free."

We all looked at him with stunned eyes as we waited for an explanation.

"Freya knew ye were nearing a plan to end Machara, and she insisted that I leave. She thought my absence would weaken her, and it seems she was right. I've had Pinkie and Davina spying on the lot of ye for weeks now, keeping me apprised of yer progress."

I glanced around the table and knew that we were all worried about the same thing. Nicol was so happy now, but he still had no idea that we'd been unable to save Freya.

Raudrich stood once again. "Nicol, 'tis true that Machara is dead but there is something else ye must know. We dinna succeed..."

Nicol interrupted him, as he called out to Pinkie in the hallway, "Pinkie, lad, what is taking ye so long with the chair? 'Tis long past time for the space at the other end of this table to be filled."

My breath caught in my chest, and I felt Marcus' hand close over my own.

It wasn't possible.

Pinkie burst through the doors, chair in tow as he apologized, "I'm sorry, sir. She couldna decide which one she wanted, insisted on trying them all out, she did."

Marcus couldn't stay silent a moment longer. "Who? Who are you talking about?"

Freya suddenly appeared in the doorway, and Marcus was out of his chair and pulling her into his arms with a speed that made me wonder if all of the men had been playing possum for days just to get some extra sympathy from all of us for their big sacrifice.

"Freya, where have you been? I thought…I didn't think it worked."

He picked her up and spun her around as she laughed.

It was the strangest thing to see her whole after only seeing her ghost for so many months.

"I'm so sorry, lad, but Nicol insisted on it. If ye succeeded in saving me, he wanted me to himself for just a wee bit of time."

He set her down and frowned at her. "So, you've been here all this time?"

"Aye. The moment the spell was cast, I returned to my body once more. Pinkie quickly whisked me away to the inn in the village where Nicol awaited me."

I could tell by Marcus' expression that part of him wanted to be angry with her, but he was too relieved to have her back to scold her in any way.

It didn't take long for the rest of the table to surround her, covering her in hugs and affection.

For the first time in decades, it seemed that all the sorrow was gone from Castle Murray.

*W*hen we woke the next morning, I found a note slipped under the door of what was now Marcus' and my shared cabin.

All it said was, "*Tell Laurel thank you. Yours, Ross.*"

He'd left in the night to start again in Boston.

CHAPTER 44

March 1653

No one was in any real rush to decide what came next for everyone. All of Castle Murray's residents were just so glad to have Freya back that we were all content to enjoy the a few months of leisure.

It didn't take long after things were settled for Olivia to give her full heart to Jimmie. I expected to hear news of their engagement any day.

I smiled as Marcus walked over to me in the garden as I worked the flowers that were now much more difficult to keep alive.

"Guess what?"

I stood and turned toward his embrace. "What?"

"Laurel's pregnant."

Marcus' excitement was palpable. Laurel was basically his sister. It meant he would soon be an uncle.

"Is she?"

He nodded and lifted my chin to kiss me. "Mmm hmm. I can't wait to put a baby in you."

I laughed. "Let's get the wedding in June under our belt first, okay? I have a very specific vision of what I want to look like when I walk down the aisle to you, and it doesn't involve my belly reaching you before the rest of me does."

"Okay," he sighed playfully. "I have a feeling Nicol has come to a decision about things around here. He's just sent word that he wishes to speak to everyone over dinner tonight."

I had a sneaking suspicion that I already knew what Nicol was going to announce, but I kept my hunch to myself as I hugged Marcus.

If I was right, Nicol and Freya would be leaving us soon, and I wasn't all that eager to spoil Marcus' good mood.

*N*icol waited until the end of dinner to make his announcement.

"Each of ye lads canna know the debt I owe ye. If I live to be one hundred, I will never be able to repay ye for the sacrifices ye have made for me, but I shall do what I can to show ye how grateful I am.

"Freya and I have spent a great deal of time deciding what we want over these last few months, and we have finally come to an agreement—one I hope that each of ye will respect and honor.

"I am selling Castle Murray to Raudrich. The castle and this isle shall be his to keep and serve. As for the rest of ye, ye will each have more money to yer name than ye shall ever need in yer lifetime. I hope ye will take it and use it to tend to the people around ye and to start anew. Yer lives are now yers to do with as ye please. I only mean to help ye along with it.

"As for my wife and me, we have purchased a small cottage in the village and are happy to live there in simple contentment for the rest of our days together."

I sighed in relief for Marcus. At least Freya would only be a short horse ride away.

I looked around at the faces of the men who for so long had believed this was the only life they would ever know. Tears shown in many of their eyes.

I couldn't wait to see what would become of each of them. I knew without a doubt they wouldn't squander Nicol's gift.

They'd all missed so much time already.

CHAPTER 45

One Month Later – April 1653

Nicol's announcement shifted things in the castle quickly. With the resources to begin anew, all of the men really began to think about what they wanted the next chapter of their lives to look like. Kate assured everyone that when Paton's time in the land of the Fae came to an end, she and the rest at Castle Murray would be there to help him rehabilitate back to everyday life. While Maddock and Marcus would stay on at the castle to live and work with Raudrich, Marcus and I knew it wouldn't be long before the group began to break up and transition into their new and separate lives.

We couldn't imagine getting married without any of them.

And so...with no magic to aid us, we enlisted the help of those around us and worked around the clock for the better part of the next thirty days to move our June wedding up to April.

Kate had been all too happy to turn the castle's dining hall into a ballroom like I'd never seen before.

Myla worked nonstop to make me a dress that rivaled anything I'd seen in the twenty-first century.

Jimmie and Brachan rode together to Allen territory to gather my dad and Leanna so they could be here for the wedding, as well. What they didn't yet know was that they were going to be surprised with a second wedding just three days after my own.

I made Marcus sleep in his bedroom inside the castle for the fortnight leading up to our wedding day. I was losing my mind with need for him, but I knew our time apart would make our wedding night all the more spectacular.

When the morning finally came, I woke inside my cabin with Liv by my side, already awake and sitting next to me with a cup of tea in her hand.

"Do ye know what today is?"

I decided to play along with her. "Hmm...I don't know. What day is it?"

She smiled and reached out to place her palm gently on the side of my face. "Today is the day ye get to marry the man ye were meant for, Silva. All that heartache was leading ye to this, and I couldna be happier for ye."

I started to cry as emotions welled up within me, but Liv was having none of that. "No crying today. Ye doona have time for it. Laurel, Kate, Myla, Ma and Da are walking up the pathway as we speak. Ye willna have a moment to cry once they get here. Best ye take a deep breath now, for the day will fly by for ye, I'm sure."

And it did.

We skipped our own wedding reception. Of course we stayed long enough to dole out hugs and to cut our cake, but the moment the music began to play and our loved ones began to mingle, I felt Marcus tug on my hand. We escaped the castle and headed to our favorite place—the garden.

He had candles lit everywhere, and the full moon could be seen through the garden's glass ceiling.

"Did you do all of this?"

He nodded and pulled me into his arms. We danced to the sounds of running water and croaking frogs.

"I did. This is where I fell in love with you, Silva, that first night when I asked you to dance and pulled you into my arms. The moment I wrapped my arms around you, I could see my whole future."

I laughed as I allowed my head to fall against his chest as he spun me around the garden pathways. "You couldn't possibly have seen that then."

"But I did. And then when you were gone so quickly after that night together, I thought perhaps I was crazy, but I wasn't. Things were just going to take a little more time than I hoped."

"I love you, Marcus."

"Oh, Silva. You've made me the man I've always wanted to be. I'm so glad that I get to spend my life by your side."

The party could go on all night without us if it wanted.

We were both exactly where we wanted to be.

EPILOGUE

*A*ugust 1653

*W*e waited until summer to take our honeymoon. We wanted it to be warm and green so we could sleep out under the stars as much as possible.

It didn't surprise me that by the time Marcus and I arrived back at Castle Murray after our extended summer-long adventure that a letter awaited me with Ross' handwriting. Somehow I'd known he would hear about the wedding, and no matter how much pain I knew it caused him, he would feel obligated to wish me well.

I imagined he still held on to far too much guilt over how he'd handled things to let the day pass for me unacknowledged.

"Ross?"

I nodded as Marcus walked up behind me, wrapping his arms around my waist as he cradled the small bump that we'd yet to tell anyone else about. We planned to share our happy news at dinner. With Laurel ready to burst and Kate halfway there as well, it seemed that Castle Murray would soon be filled with babies. That would undoubtedly keep everyone on their toes.

I had, however, sent word to my father, and he, Leanna, and all of my half siblings were already on their way to The Isle for an extended visit until after the baby was born.

Shortly after Nicol and Freya left to build their new life together and so many of The Eight had left to pursue their newfound freedom, Raudrich worried that the castle would seem far too empty. Little did he know just how intent the women of Castle Murray were on seeing the castle halls populated. If we all kept up at this pace, it wouldn't be too long before we had to build even more cabins out back.

I wiggled the still-unopened letter in my hands as I looked up at Marcus.

"Do you want to read it with me? I don't mind if you do."

He stepped away, shook his head, and smiled. He knew he'd won. Ross was no longer of any concern to him.

"No. I know that he will always hold part of your heart, and I'm okay with that. I'm the one who gets to share my life with you. I'll leave you alone so you can read whatever he has to say. I'm sure he just means to wish you well."

I waited until Marcus disappeared from the garden before I settled down on one of the benches near my favorite fountain. The garden felt different now, lighter somehow, without Freya's presence. All the joy she'd given the space remained, but it was as if even the flowers were happy to see her gone from this place and returned to her human life.

Sighing, I carefully opened the letter and bent my head to read. I could hear his voice, his thick Scottish brogue, slightly more slurred than usual from drink as I read the letter in my mind.

Silva, lass,

   Boston is sweltering in summer. Much like those July nights we spent in NYC, but I know I shouldn't speak to you of such things now. I knew even as I held you in my arms that last time that you would never truly be mine again, but I would've taken any minute I could get with you. I would have let you pretend you loved me still forever if it meant I could be near you. That selfishness in me is why you deserve far better than I could ever give you.

I suppose it was only a matter of time before he made you his wife. Only a fool would do otherwise.

I want you to know that I'm happy for you. My own broken heart will be able to keep beating because I know you are loved and cared for.

I don't suppose I'll ever see you again, but know that wherever you are, even decades from now, I'll be thinking of you still, holding you close to my heart, and hoping you are as happy then as you are now.

Always yours,

Ross

Tears ran down my face as I closed his letter and held it against my chest. There was so much I could say to him, but I was familiar enough with grief to know that until time completed its work on his heart, he wouldn't believe me anyway.

Instead, I pictured him in my mind as I whispered what I knew in my heart, hoping with every word that somehow it would travel across the centuries to him and that someday he would know the truth in my words.

"You'll always love me, yes, but Ross, my darling Ross, one day I'll only occupy the small space in your heart saved for the happy memory of us. If I was truly meant to be yours, I'd be yours still. There's another on her way to you. You don't have to believe it. Just don't shut down so much that you aren't able to let her in. Just hold on. I'm sending you all my love. Today, tomorrow, always."

I wouldn't write back to Ross. My words would do him no good, but I knew there was another letter I'd be writing that night.

One to a witch I'd only met once, one to ask for a little help for a man I would always love.

If Marcus was right about her, I was certain Morna would be up to the task.

THE END

READ ALL THE BOOKS IN MORNA'S
LEGACY. SERIES

Love Beyond Time (Book 1)
Love Beyond Reason (Book 2)
A Conall Christmas - A Novella (Book 2.5)
Love Beyond Hope (Book 3)
Love Beyond Measure (Book 4)
In Due Time – A Novella (Book 4.5)
Love Beyond Compare (Book 5)
Love Beyond Dreams (Book 6)
Love Beyond Belief (Book 7)
A McMillan Christmas - A Novella (Book 7.5)
Love Beyond Reach (Book 8)
Morna's Magic & Mistletoe - A Novella (Book 8.5)
Love Beyond Words (Book 9)
Love Beyond Wanting (Book 10)
The Haunting of Castle Dune - A Novella (Book 10.5)
Love Beyond Destiny (Book 11)

And More to Come...

SWEET/CLEAN VERSIONS OF MORNA'S LEGACY SERIES

If you enjoy sweet/clean romances where the love scenes are left behind closed doors or if you know someone else who does, check out the new sweet/clean versions of Morna's Legacy books in the Magical Matchmaker's Legacy.

Morna's Spell
Sweet/Clean Version of *Love Beyond Time*

Morna's Secret
Sweet/Clean Version of *Love Beyond Reason*

The Conall's Magical Yuletide
Sweet/Clean Version of *A Conall Christmas*

Morna's Accomplice
Sweet/Clean Version of *Love Beyond Measure*

Jeffrey's Only Wish
Sweet/Clean Version of *In Due Time*

Morna's Rogue
Sweet/Clean Version of *Love Beyond Compare*

Morna's Ghost
Sweet/Clean Version of *Love Beyond Dreams*

SUBSCRIBE TO BETHANY'S MAILING LIST

When you sign up for my mailing list, you will be the first to know about new releases, upcoming events, and contests. You will also get sneak peeks into books and have opportunities to participate in special reader groups and occasionally get codes for free books.

Just go to my website (www.bethanyclaire.com) and click the Mailing List link in the header. I can't wait to connect with you there.

ABOUT THE AUTHOR

BETHANY CLAIRE is a USA Today bestselling author of swoon-worthy, Scottish romance and time travel novels. Bethany loves to immerse her readers in worlds filled with lush landscapes, hunky Scots, lots of magic, and happy endings.

She has two ornery fur-babies, plays the piano every day, and loves Disney and yoga pants more than any twenty-something really should. She is most creative after a good night's sleep and the perfect cup of tea. When not writing, Bethany travels as much as she possibly can, and she never leaves home without a good book to keep her company.

If you want to read more about Bethany or if you're curious about when her next book will come out, please visit her website at: www.bethanyclaire.com, where you can sign up to receive email notifications about new releases.

ACKNOWLEDGMENTS

Firstly, to my readers. I know this one was a doozy of a wait. Thanks so for much for hanging in there and for returning to this world after so much time.

To Rori Bumgarner, Karen Corboy, Elizabeth Halliday, Johnetta Ivey, Vivian Nwankpah, and Pamela Oviatt, you ladies are Rock Stars. Thank you for continually coming back for more.

To Mom and Maegan, I know that I don't thank you guys enough. I'm not sure I would be able to put up with me the way you guys do. I really am so grateful. I love you both more than you'll ever know.

67318850R00161